WITHOUT FEAR OR FAVOUR

AND OTHER STORIES

STEPHEN COLLIER

Stephen Collier JAN 25

eBook: ISBN 9781739444228
Paperback: ISBN 9781739444235

Stephen Collier Ltd
Five-2-Eight Media
Dodford, Northampton. UK
www.stephencollier.com
Email: contact@stephencollier.com

British Library Cataloguing in Publication Data
A catalogue reference for this book is available from the British Library.

INTRODUCTION

In the dark underbelly of human experience, where shadows and secrets lie buried, stories of mystery and danger await. This anthology brings together four crime fiction tales and two paranormal stories, each a journey into realms where the line between justice and breaking solemn oaths blurs and the unexplainable tugs at the edges of reality.

Here, detectives unravel impossible mysteries, and ordinary people find themselves ensnared in events far beyond their control, forced to confront the unsettling truths of the human soul. Every narrative plunges the reader deeper into a labyrinth of tension, where each plot twist exposes a new, chilling possibility.

The crime fiction stories delve into worlds ruled by betrayal and revenge. From rough cityscapes to remote villages, these stories uncover the motivations and ethical dilemmas of characters both within the law and beyond its reach.

A veteran detective wrestles with an unsolved case that resurfaces after years. A demand for sanctuary takes a deadly turn, and in the shadows, a doctor manipulates lives like pawns on a board. Each story tests the boundaries of bonds, challenging the reader to ask: how far would you go to break a solemn promise, and at what cost?

Yet even as these tales ground us in the harsh realities of crime, the paranormal stories take us to another level of intrigue, where answers are elusive, and fear creeps in like a chill at dawn. Ghostly whispers in abandoned houses, visions that defy explanation, and events that hint at an existence beyond our own make up these haunting stories.

In these narratives, the paranormal isn't merely a backdrop but a force that upends lives, leaving characters—and readers—questioning the nature of reality itself.

Together, these six stories promise an exploration of crime and the uncanny, a collection that lingers in the mind long after the final page.

Stephen Collier
Northampton
Nov 2024

1

WITHOUT FEAR OR FAVOUR

In the near future.

'Did you ever think of the consequences of stirring up hatred and resentment in your news reports?' Alex railed at his wife, a television news anchor. He continued, 'Did you not even think that society is in such a state that it was bound to make my job a damn sight harder?'

Lucy was standing, leaning up against the kitchen worktop with a glass of wine in her hand. It had been a hard day that was not being helped by the tirade from her husband of twenty years. This was not unusual. She'd heard it all before, so she let him bang on about it until he got it out of his system. She realised he was still talking.

'Are you listening to me?'

'Have you finished?' she asked with more than a touch of anger.

'I haven't even bloody started.'

'Well, let me put it like this.' She pushed herself off the work unit and walked up to him, standing toe-to-toe with her husband. Counting on her fingers, she said, 'One, I don't write the news stories. I only read them. You know that. Two, it's my role to report the news as it is, not - as you think - make it up as I go along, and three, you need to make sure that your workforce remains safe. That's your job, not mine. I only report the consequences of your ineptitude.'

She turned and walked away, thumping the glass hard on the worktop. She looked him straight in the eye, then growled, 'You can sleep on the sofa tonight,' with that, she stormed out of the kitchen. 'I'm going to bed.'

Alex heard her climb the stairs and enter the bathroom, where the door slammed. He downed the few dregs left in his whiskey glass, grabbed the bottle from the side, and slumped down on the sofa in the living room, a minimalist space with a 60-inch TV on the wall over the pseudo-fireplace.

'TV on.' The screen surged into life. 'Open UKN News.' The TV channel changed to the UK Network News.

The evening news anchor, Barry Banks, ran through the day's highlights, banging on about something, but Alex wasn't listening. He was more concerned about what the County Commander would say during his morning meeting with her. That would be difficult and exacerbated because his wife was the reporter who broke the story. 'I'll be accused, no doubt, of giving her the info,' he grumbled into his whiskey glass before taking a gulp. 'TV off,' he hissed. The screen went black. Standing, he walked over to where he had dropped his bag when he got home and recovered his tablet. A thin sliver of electronics that belied its power to connect to the rest of the world. He sat on the sofa and opened the file on what had caused such a stir early in his day.

The incident summary was incomplete—it was just a precis of the circumstances. But Alex knew more. After reading through the summary and the report he had received from the duty inspector, he re-enacted the incident in his mind.

It started with a message to PC Khan, sent to his car's tablet. It read:

Report of street fighting at the Meadowcroft Lane private estate. Suspected anti-establishment involvement. Be careful. - Control - Timed 1946.

Khan had responded positively and made his way. He'd taken fifteen minutes to get there. He probably hoped it had all dispersed by the time he arrived. Run to a fire, walk to a fight, was what he had always been told. He'd recorded his arrival with control via his tablet at 20:05.

PC KHAN STOPPED his patrol car at the end of the road. It was dark. No streetlights were on. This part of the city was in blackout time, blacked out on a rota to conserve energy. There was always some anti-social behaviour at these blackout locations, so PC Khan had no real problem. He'd dealt with it before. He'll deal with it again.

Khan was a naturalised immigrant from Afghanistan who served as an interpreter with the British Army. He was one of the lucky ones who left the country when the British and Americans withdrew. He finally brought his wife and child over and was the happiest he'd ever been doing the job he loved. Not only was he an interpreter, but he was also an Afghan policeman before the country went south.

At nearly forty years old, he had black swept-back hair, a closely cropped full beard, and deep-blue eyes - unusual for a man of his ethnic origin.

Knowing about recent intelligence regarding these reports,

he unclipped his sidearm and rested his hand on the grip of his H&K pistol - just in case.

His fight-or-flight mode racked up several notches as he exited the car. Checking he'd adjusted his body armour correctly, he stepped forward. He took two paces. The sting in his arm came as a shot rang out, reverberating around the estate. He fell to his knees. The coup de grâce entered his temple and blew out the opposite side of his face. He was dead before the bullet had exited his head.

ALEX SIGHED HEAVILY. The growing anarchist movements in the country since the collapse of the third coalition government in a decade remained a significant concern for the security of the nation and an even more critical concern for his policing division with its large ethnic community. Democracy had broken down. Various factions now controlled parts of the country in a disjointed kingdom that harked back to the days of King Ethelbert in AD794. Policing divisions had become small enforcement bailiwicks in their own rights, controlled by officers like Alex as pseudo-chief constables. There was no cohesive enforcement between the divisions, and the tensions within his own were high.

The constant media barrage on anti-migrant communities did not help the situation. And his wife seemed to be the main protagonist when she was on air. Her argument had always been that bad people needed to be called out. But that also included whatever was happening with the new National Police Service. Divisional commanders were each vying for political acceptance by whatever political faction appeared to be in control of their division.

Some of his colleagues in other divisions ruled with an iron fist, and some divisions were almost always in a state of martial law. He did not subscribe to this attitude and believed in the freedom of the masses but drew the line at anarchy.

Now, he was going to have to deal with a group of individuals who shot and killed one of his officers. His struggles were only starting.

The following morning, he went to his office. He didn't speak to his wife. She'd already left for her early morning show by the time he got up. He'd slept in the spare room. A night on the sofa was unconscionable.

On his way to the office, the County Commander (CC) (previously known as a chief constable) rang him—no niceties from her.

'Where are you?' she asked.

'On my way into my office.'

'Good, you know we have a problem with this assassination of one of our officers.'

'Tell me something I don't already know.' If she was going to be curt, so could he.

'Well, your bloody missus has stirred up a shit storm this morning, banging on about the type of officers we recruit and our inability to find who did it.'

Alex wanted to defend his wife but knew the CC was correct and said nothing.

The commander continued, 'Not only that, but she advocated other organisations do our job for us.'

Alex stared out the car window at the passing traffic and said nothing.

'I need you to sort this out before your division becomes a bloody laughingstock.'

'Yes, ma'am.'

'Any idea?'

'No - just the usual suspects.'

5

'Well, pull them all in, give them a shake and see what falls out.'

'Might be difficult. We don't even know who they all are.'

'Bloody well find out then. Report to me by the end of the day. I want a result.'

She hung up. 'Fucking idiot,' Alex mumbled. The County Commander used to be called the Police and Crime Commissioner. Her role remained political and not operational. There was, therefore, a complete misunderstanding of the roles in both directions. Alex wasn't a political animal. He just wanted to get his job done and return to the way things were before this collapse started without being interrupted by people who knew fuck all about the job.

His driver parked the car under the HQ canopy, and he got out, heading for the lift to the third floor. Striding towards his office, DCI Max Freestone joined him.

'Well?' was all that Alex said.

'Needle in a haystack, boss. It is nigh on impossible to get any info out of anyone. No witnesses. House to house - nobody heard a thing. Lights were out, nobody saw anything.'

'Hmm. Just had the CC on the phone. She's not happy.'

'Whenever is she?' Max smiled.

They entered Alex's airy, windowed office, which he always thought was too big for one person, but it came with the job. 'Computer on,' he said as he entered. The ultra-thin computer on his desk fired up silently and automatically followed his eyeline, so he had a full-screen view anywhere he looked. The latest computer technology virtually took over everyone's life.

'Open Incident 850 of yesterday.'

The computer complied, and documents relating to the death of his officer appeared on the screen.

'Have we got the PM report yet?' Max asked.

'Show PM report 850 dash one.'

The report appeared on the screen. They both studied it. Max pointed to the report and said, 'He was shot twice.'

'Seems so.'

'Why? Why not just take him out with one kill shot?'

'I'd had the same thought.'

According to CCTV, PC Khan fell to his knees after the first shot.

'Then the second shot came a few seconds later.'

'Perhaps it was all about him needing to be in a kneeling position before the last shot. A short time to pray to his God or whatever.'

'Like an old-style execution?'

Max nodded. There was a knock on the door. They both turned to see a young detective constable standing there.

'Come in,' Alex said.

'I thought you might like to know, sir, but you need to switch on the TV.'

Alex looked towards the TV on the wall. An older model that still used a remote. He switched it on. The news channel flicked into life. UKNN provided twenty-four-hour rolling news, or, as Alex thought, brainwashing. Scrolling news picked up on anything that could be true or fake from personal media channels, like "Mylifebook".

The face of his wife filled the screen. Alex groaned. 'What the fuck is she stirring up now?' Nobody answered. It seemed impolite to do so.

'There's been some criticism of our methods,' the DC said.

'Why am I not surprised?' Max said.

The DC left as the two senior officers sat down to listen to what was being said.

'Here are today's headlines. I'm Lucy Hawkesworth,' Lucy said, smiling. 'The Western Police Command are still reeling from the death of one of their officers yesterday, but there is still no news about how the investigation is progressing.'

'Why would we want to tell them, anyway?' Max said.

'They need info to slag us off, as usual,' Alex said.

'Despite police command not being able to discover who the group is, UKNN has, with our great investigative resources of our own, found a witness to the entire event.'

Both men sat up at that news.

'The witness we have disguised from fear of retribution.' A darkened scene came on the screen with a person in silhouette. 'Adam reports.'

The screen changed to a man standing outside police headquarters. Talking directly to the camera, he said, 'Investigations into the death of a young Muslim police officer continue by our own investigation unit. Despite the police denying that there are no witnesses to the event, our investigations have found a witness who saw everything.' The screen changed back to the dark-screened silhouette. A voice came on the screen with a caption read, "Voice disguised".

'What happened last night?' Adam said.

'Well, the copper came round into the estate, screeched to a stop. He got out with his gun in his hand and seemed to shoot at something, then he fell down when he was himself shot.'

'Thank you for that info, which we've passed on to the police. Back to you in the studio.'

Alex clicked the TV off and threw the remote into a chair.

'Who is this witness, Max? Because clearly, he's talking a load of bollocks. Did they hand us his details?'

'We have received nothing from anyone at UKNN. And as we've seen the real CCTV footage, the only thing we've got him on is false statements.'

'Well, you better find who the hell they were talking to, where he is now, and get that fucking reporter in as well.'

'Okay, boss.' And with that, Max left.

Alex sat heavily in the chair behind his desk and rubbed his face. Taking a moment, he leaned back and observed the fast-moving, thick clouds through the window. Leaning forward, he picked up his phone and dialled a number. The call was answered immediately.

'Didn't think it would be long before you rang,' the male voice on the other end of the phone said.

'Do you know who did this?'

'No.'

'Can you find out?'

'No.'

'Why?'

'Bit close to home.'

'Meaning?'

No reply. 'Well?'

'Well, what?'

'Look, you gonna tell me who did this, or do I have to come round there and beat it out of you?'

There was a chuckle from the phone. 'Huh. You can try. As I said, it's a bit close to home.'

'And how am I supposed to do anything with that buggeration of info?'

'You'll soon find out.'

'What does that mean? You have anything to do with that lying little toerag of a witness?'

'Maybe.'

'Fuck's sake - and you take it to the press before coming to us?'

'They pay better.' The phone went dead.

Alex looked at his handset and then chucked it down as well. What a brilliant fucking day he was having!

~

It was three days before any further information was forthcoming about the death of PC Khan.

Alex was sitting at home in the evening. He still hadn't made it up with his wife about the way she reported the news on TV and the innuendo they put on what and how they said it. In fact, he was feeling more and more concerned about her entire attitude towards the police and society. It was as if she was believing her own propaganda.

His phone rang, and he saw it was his DCI.

'What's up, Max?'

'Just had some info into the perps for Khan's murder.'

'Oh.' He sat up. 'And what's that? I hope it's good news?'

'I suppose that depends on your point of view.'

'Do you need me to come in?'

'It might be wise – the CC is here.'

'The fuck does she want?'

'Doesn't speak with minions like me.' He chuckled.

'OK. Stay there, I'll be in in thirty.' He hung up.

There was no response from Lucy. Alex thought she was in her home studio doing some recordings and knew not to interrupt. Well, she'd find out he wasn't there later.

Alex shrugged on his coat and made his way to his office. When he got there, the CC was sitting behind his desk. She didn't stand when he came in and didn't offer to move from behind his desk.

'What news from the front, ma'am?' Alex tried to make light. He'd always been a bit of a history buff.

The CC just glowered at him. Max was sitting in one of the office chairs, scrolling on his phone. He turned to him.

'Come on then, Max. I'm sure neither of you has brought

me here just for the good of my health at this time of the evening.'

Before Max could reply, the CC said, 'I think we have our shooter.'

'Really?' questioned Alex.

Max stood up and walked over to the both of them. The CC pushed the monitor towards them.

'This guy is currently in custody.' She showed him the custody photo. Dark, shoulder-length hair, two to three days' growth, about 40 years old.

'Okay, so what's he got to say for himself?'

'He said,' Max began, 'that he knew who shot PC Khan.'

'And did he say who, and have we arrested him yet?'

'Apparently, he won't say until he's spoken to you,' the CC said. 'Do you know him?'

He did, but he would not give her the satisfaction of that. Alex shook his head. 'Doesn't look familiar. How did we pick him up?'

'Drink drive,' Max said. 'RCU picked him up - ran a red light.'

Figures thought Alex. 'And he wants to speak with me?'

'Yeah, but he's too pissed now to talk to anyone.'

I bet.

Finally, the CC stood up, straightened her tunic and stepped out from behind Alex's desk.

'Well, I expect a result when you do speak with him.'

'Ma'am.'

She left Alex and Max.

'Fucking cheek of the woman,' Alex said, going behind his desk, now vacated by the CC.

'What would she say to me if I went and sat behind her desk?'

'Perhaps you ought to find out.' Max grinned. 'So, what have we got on this guy, and why does he want to talk to you?'

'He's a minor villain in town – drugs, contraband, that sort of thing. He'd have been called a 'spiv' in the 1940s.'

'You do know him, then.'

Alex nodded. 'Yeah, he's a snitch.'

'Ah, understood.'

'Is he really off his face?'

'Yup.'

'Okay, we'll talk to him in the morning. I'm going home.'

'Drink first,' Max said.

Alex thought for a moment. 'Mind if I join you?'

'WHAT DID you want to tell me?' Alex had opened the cell door where 'Faisal the Filcher' had spent the night. The place smelt like a whore's brothel.

'That copper who got shot.'

Alex stepped into the cell with Max behind him.

'What about him?'

'I may know what happened?'

'You better tell me, then.'

'That depends.'

'On what?'

'What deal we're gonna make?'

'No deal, Faisal. You tell me, and I'll see what I can do. No promises.'

Faisal shook his head. 'Gotta be more than promises. This is premium information.'

They stared at each other, then Alex turned to go.

'Wait!'

Alex turned back. 'Changed your mind?'

'Okay, only because it's my civic duty to tell you what I know.'

'Since when have you had a civic conscience?'

'Always. You know that.'

'Go on then, tell me.'

The information passed to Alex by Faisal was indeed gold dust. And extremely explosive. True to his word, Alex arranged for Faisal's release without charge on the proviso that they would add it back on the charge sheet if he got caught again - for any offence.

Walking back to his office, Alex had time to assimilate the information. Faisal had never provided duff info on anything he'd asked him for, but this information seemed too farfetched to be true. If it was, he could have a full-scale riot on his hands and on his patch.

There was no way he could go to the CC with this information. It could blow the entire game. But he needed to tell somebody he could trust, which was a big ask.

'Faisal the Filcher' smiled as he left the police station without charge. He'd done what he'd been told to do. He'd given his 'handler' what he was told to give, and now he was a free man and soon to be a rich man.

Unable to take his car, he left the station grounds and walked down the hill on his way home, feeling happy. Thinking about what he wanted to do with his extra money. No one had ever given him so much for doing so little.

He walked on, crossing a duelled main road and turned left towards his flat. The area where he lived was in a run-down condition. There hadn't been a rubbish collection for weeks. Rats and urban foxes had ripped bags open.

The sun was setting, and he needed to be inside his flat before the curfew imposed by the current political group running the area.

He walked towards the entrance to his flat. A solid white door with several doorbells on both sides of the framework.

As he put his PIN into the lock, a man stepped out of the shadows and approached him. Faisal didn't see the gun until it was too late, darting to the right in the hope the bullet wouldn't hit anything vital. But he wasn't quick enough and fell to the ground. The man said nothing and walked on as surrounding neighbours came out of their houses and apartments to see what was happening.

The ambulance took Faisal, unconscious but not dead, to the hospital.

A TEAM OF ASSEMBLED OFFICERS, led by DCI Freestone, stood at the threshold of the house they were about to raid. With the information supplied by Faisal, the raid aimed to arrest the occupants. Max thought that if the information was good, they could clear up this whole mess.

The house was on a well-to-do estate, set in larger than average grounds. Lots of places to hide. It had a nice front door, which was a pity, as it was going to be battered down any minute.

When everyone was in place, Max ordered them to go in. Using a chainsaw, they sliced their way into the house, surprising the occupants.

They were all in the main room with papers - unusual today - spread across the table. The house owner stood up abruptly.

'What is the meaning of this?' the owner called to Max, who had entered the room after the uniformed officers.

'We have a warrant to search the premises for information about the death of a police constable five days ago. You'll all be taken into custody.' He indicated to the officers to take all four people away. Max thought to himself that the boss wouldn't approve of this.

ALEX'S MEETING with his counterparts on other divisions following the raid didn't go well. Revelations about what happened on the raid and who got arrested made an already volatile situation even more tense.

The Eastern Command Chief Superintendent spoke first.

'Perhaps it would have been prudent to let us all in on what was happening, Alex. We may have been able to help.'

'Look, I didn't even know what we were likely to find. The information we received was third-hand, and it was just that those who had orchestrated the attack on my officer would all be at the address. That was the only intelligence we had.'

'Why not wait for more intelligence?' Eastern asked.

'I could see why,' the Southern Commander said. 'Strike while the iron was hot and all that.'

'Something like that, yes,' Alex said.

'What about the Watch committee?' the Northern Commander asked. 'Have you notified them?'

'Not told them yet.'

'Probably best. Wouldn't you agree, everyone?'

'They have no power over what we tell them, anyway,' the Eastern Commander said.

'That's agreed, then,' Alex said. A nodding of heads and an agreement to detain without charge, indefinitely, those arrested in the raid under the old terrorism laws until the actual shooter of PC Khan was apprehended.

Max had been sitting outside the meeting room when his phone pinged him a message:

CONTACT COUNTY HOSPITAL. ASAP. INFO ON OFFICER DEATH. CONTROL.

Max wondered what that was all about, so he stood by the window to get a better signal. Reinforced concrete structures were renowned for acting like a Faraday cage, preventing signals from getting in or out. He leaned against the window frame and was about to dial the hospital when Alex came out of his meeting.

'How was it, then?' he asked.

'As you'd expect. Commanders feathering their own nests in the hope of further promotion if they got this right.'

'And you?'

'What about me.'

'Was anything said about ... you know.'

'A few mentioned it, but most seemed to realise it was inevitable at some stage.'

'Yeah, they've all been caught out at one time.'

'You got a message?' pointing at Max's phone.

'Er, yeah, something about contacting the hospital for info about the case.'

'Right then, let's drop in on the way past.'

Back in the car, Alex said, 'What the hell am I going to do now?'

'The information, if it's correct, is going to upset many people.'

'I'll admit I have a dilemma, Max.'

'You've never been one for shirking your responsibility, Alex, but as you say, a tough decision will have to be made.'

'Okay, when we get back to the nick, send some officers to make those two extra arrests, then I think we'll gather them all together and put this matter to rest once and for all.'

'THIS IS HIGHLY IRREGULAR, SIR,' the custody sergeant said to Alex.

'I know, but if we want to find out who killed our officer and who organised it, these people know who did it or were complicit in its action.'

'I understand - but you know who we've got locked up here, so I need to go by the book.'

'Look, Sergeant, if it's any consolation, this is all on my head if it goes south. You have nothing to worry about – you acted on my instructions.'

'Can I have that in writing?' He smiled.

Alex responded with a reciprocal smile. 'Get them all into the conference room, then station two armed officers on the door.'

The custody sergeant nodded his agreement.

'And keep a firearms team close by as well. Just in case.'

'I'll let you know when they're all ready, sir. And on your head be it.'

'Thank you, Sergeant.'

Alex left the custody suite and returned to his office. When he arrived, the Eastern Commander was already in his office.

'What's this all about, Alex?' he said as Alex entered.

'You'll need to join us in the conference room in ten minutes to find that out. I don't really know myself yet.'

'But you have some ideas. Some evidence.'

'Plenty of evidence, yes. Plenty of other ideas as well.'

'And this is all about the death of PC Khan?'

Alex nodded.

'Christ, Alex. This will not look good in the press, will it?'

'As far as I can make out, it's all down to the press stirring up hatred in the first place.'

'Yeah, but there is a big difference between reporting the news and making it.'

'Even so ...'

Alex's phone rang. He answered it. Said nothing and cleared the call.

'Okay, they're ready.'

~

ALEX ENTERED THE CONFERENCE ROOM, guarded by armed officers. There was no way he was going to give six people involved in a conspiracy to kill a police officer any opportunity to leg it out the door.

A thought entered his mind as he looked upon the six. *If the devil could cast his net now!* He smiled inwardly as he took his place standing at the head of the conference room table.

The officer deployed to stand guard remained in the room in front of the door. The only way in or out of the room. Unless, of course, you were desperate enough to throw yourself out of the window.

The room was quiet – forty-eight hours in a cell usually had that effect. And he knew that one of the six pulled the trigger that killed PC Khan. He already had a good idea who, but would not let on just yet. Alex wanted to understand the motivation for this crime.

Alex began. 'You may think it is unorthodox to gather suspects together in one room to talk about this crime, like an Agatha Christie novel or even an old *Death in Paradise* episode.' Someone spoke, but he shut them down. 'My aim of gathering you all together in the same room is to elicit information. You have information that involves you all, completely or partially. Whatever the case, someone in this room killed PC Khan.' Alex meandered around the room, looking at those assembled and glancing out of the window at a leaden sky. Turning back to them, he said, 'Someone actually pulled the trigger, not once but twice. Someone set him up. Someone made the police service look incompetent. I have been a police officer for over thirty years. In that time, I dealt with corruption both within the organisation and local government, and what happened to PC Khan brought us all closer to anarchy, which some wanted but most did not. So whatever happens here, now, whoever speaks first to put this matter to rest, the outcome will be the same and not good for any of you.'

Alex looked around the room at the six in front of him. They were Lucy Hawkesworth - his wife; Billy Banks - TV newscaster and producer; the County Commander and her staff officer; and the two thugs arrested on Faisal's evidence that morning.

The County Commander spoke first. 'This is an outrageous affront to both me and my staff officer. You've not spoken to me since your illegal raid on my house, or the damage you've done to my front door, making these arrests null and void ...'

Alex held up his hand to shut her up. 'With respect, ma'am, if you resort to illegal activities and abuse of your power, you deserve to get your door bashed in.'

The County Commander huffed and puffed. 'How dare you speak to me in that tone; I am your superior officer ...'

'Just shut up, Linda. Superior?' He chuckled. 'No – only my boss, for now. Let me tell you what I know to be true.' He turned his attention to Billy Banks. 'It started a long time ago, didn't it, Billy?'

Billy remained silent, staring straight ahead.

'A revenge for the death of your son, by a person not of your faith and who is now in prison for life. But you were not happy with that, were you, Billy, and exacted your revenge. But you couldn't do it alone, could you?'

Still, he remained silent.

'So, you took advantage of your friendship with my wife to get in touch with the County Commander to hatch your revenge plan. I wondered why you would want to involve her, but then you two also have a history. But that's for later.

'All three of you hatched a plan to murder a police officer in cold blood, then manipulate the news into making people think it was the police's fault for not protecting their own.'

'That's an outright lie, Alex.' Lucy fumed, enraged by Alex's comments.

'Is it, though? Your actions and demeanour at home would tell me differently. Ever since the death of PC Khan, you've been on edge, fractious, argumentative.'

'Maybe so, but you haven't been such a shining light yourself, Alex.'

'I'm not getting into a domestic argument here and now. I'll continue.

'Despite Billy wanting the revenge he sought, the only person who could mastermind such a plot was my boss, here. The County Commander.'

'Another lie,' the CC seethed.

'Not so.' He indicated to the officer on the door, who opened it. He called in a young woman who'd been waiting outside the room.

'Your PA, I believe?'

The CC nodded. Turning to the young PA, he said, 'Would you tell me, please, about the communication you intercepted, unintentionally, two days before PC Khan's murder.'

Looking nervous, the PA was about to speak but was interrupted by the CC's staff officer.

'There is no need to put her through this, Chief Superintendent. I will tell you what she knows.'

The CC shot him an 'I dare you' glance.

'Very well.' Alex dismissed the PA, turning his attention to the staff officer.

'You say anything and it'll be the last thing you ever do for me,' the CC growled.

Alex said, 'With the information I have on both of you, it will be. Now. Tell me.'

Ignoring comments made by CC, the staff officer began.

'Your wife – who wanted to introduce Mr Banks to the CC, not knowing there was already a connection there – contacted us. I thought it would be for just another TV interview, so I allowed the PA to put the CC in touch with him.

'I was not party to all their conversations, but the CC took me into her confidence on a matter I first thought was a joke.'

'And that joke was?' Alex said.

'A revenge killing of a police officer.'

'Why?'

'Because you couldn't investigate your way out of a paper bag, that's why,' Lucy butt in.

'I'll come to your role in a minute. Until he's finished, keep quiet.'

Lucy folded her arms and huffed like a petulant child.

'Go on, please.'

'I asked the CC why we would want to do this but was told to just get on and follow her orders.'

'Which were?'

The staff officer looked towards the two thugs at the end of the table. 'To find them.'

'And how did you do that?'

'Before I was a staff officer, I was undercover on several

major enquiries, where naturally one comes into contact with such people who fit the bill as to what the CC wanted.'

'All for the revenge of one man?'

The staff officer nodded.

'What have you got to say for yourself, Commander?'

'Our role in this county differs from elsewhere.'

'Well, that's tripe to start with. What made the both of you give up on your oath?'

'Have you seen the state of the county?' the CC goaded.

'I've seen the state of the entire country. Our county is no different, and the way it's portrayed on the news channel clearly has a bias towards the anarchists.'

'That's not true,' Lucy exclaimed.

'It is, Luce.'

Billy Banks was about to speak for the first time. Lucy looked at him. 'What do you mean?'

'I attend production meetings and the like as a producer and a presenter. There is a clear bias against law and order.'

Lucy shook her head. 'Why, Billy, why?'

'We have to keep the public on our side—'

'By killing a police officer?' Lucy said, her voice rising an octave. 'What the hell have you got me into?'

'It's called perverting the course of justice and conspiracy to murder,' Alex said.

'How come?' she asked.

'Because you knew about it and didn't tell me.'

'But—'

'No buts. If you had come to me with this information when you first knew about it, all of you - especially you, Linda – could have prevented the death of a hard-working and diligent officer. But all you wanted was a good news story so you could slag us all off. I am, I have to say, disappointed with all of you. I certainly thought that you two,' pointing to the CC and her staff officer, 'had a better set of morals than you have.'

There was silence in the room.

'Who pulled the trigger on my officer, and who attempted to kill Faisal the Filcher? Who is still alive, by the way.'

The two thugs in the corner looked at each other.

'How do you think we found you two?'

'Not your best detection work, is it?' Lucy said. 'Given to you on a plate.'

Alex ignored the remark. He knew after this that his marriage was over. 'I don't suppose it matters who pulled the trigger. You're all as guilty as each other, as if every one of you were there when the trigger was pulled. You will all be charged with murder, attempted murder, and perverting the course of justice.'

'Why have you done this? Could you not have just looked the other way? One more cop death means nothing anymore. It's the time we live in.'

Alex stared at the CC in incredulity. 'Because, Linda, I did not renege on my oath as a police officer to work without fear or favour.'

The CC bowed her head as an officer approached to take her and the others away.

As Lucy passed with another officer, she turned to Alex. 'I'm sorry, Alex.'

He said nothing.

2

THE ACCIDENTAL SILENCE

Dave

'Tango Mike 4.'

'Here we go,' my crewmate said as he reached for the handset of our police radio. We were in one of the last marked police Range Rovers covering motorway duty because of the incessant rain over the past few days during the wettest summer we'd had for years.

We were on an evening shift, sitting on an observation platform almost at the limit of our southern patrol area. Regular motorway patrols had become obsolete after Highways England took over the management of the motorway infrastructure.

The new "SMART" motorway, which now covered our area, was a new experience for officers like Mark and me; we used to have a hard shoulder to clear the road quickly when necessary. That's progress, I suppose.

'Go ahead, Mike 4,' Mark said into the radio.

'I wondered how long it would be before we got a call in this weather,' I remarked.

'Mike 4, attend the report of a serious injury RTC, Northbound, marker post 224 point 6, multiple vehicles, multiple injuries, carriageway blocked, HE, ambulance and fire en route,' the radio controller informed us in that matter-of-fact way life and death situations are conveyed.

'Roger, can you let us have further details as they come in? We're state 1, northbound from the Creep.'

'Roger Mike 4. All received, will do.'

The reported collision was fifteen miles away, so I accelerated into the live traffic and slipped easily onto the carriageway, making for lane four.

The blue lights on the top and front of the patrol car reflected off the heavy rain that had begun again. A shimmering wave of blue and white as I pushed the car forward. It was like looking through a kaleidoscope.

I almost guaranteed that something would happen because it frequently does in these conditions. They reported the motorway as blocked, which meant the traffic behind the collision - the "tailback" – would build at one mile per minute.

As we raced towards the scene, with sirens and the car at full throttle, we came upon the end of the tailback, some seven miles from the collision. We were still in the offside lane, where we had been since the beginning of our journey, and now we wove our way through the stationary traffic. Vehicles parted for us like the Red Sea as we struggled through a collection of cars, buses and trucks, crawling our way forward to whatever awaited us. This was the problem with these so-called "SMART" motorways. There was no way to get to the scene in a hurry if you were approaching from behind.

I could see that we were getting close. Many drivers were

already out of their cars, wanting to see what the holdup was. By this time, the rain had stopped, but the air was thick and muggy as night drew in on this late August Friday.

We stopped our patrol car, straddling the third and fourth lanes at a forty-five-degree angle between a Traffic Officer HE vehicle already on the scene and the stationary traffic.

When the motorway gets completely blocked, incidents like these allow emergency vehicles to approach by driving the wrong way down the motorway. We saw the fire brigade and more ambulances being escorted by HE coming towards us.

As I got out of the driver's seat, another ambulance was appearing from the stationary traffic. The road was a mess. A lorry and trailer had overturned and ploughed into the central reservation. The lorry cab was on its side in the fourth lane of the opposite carriageway, and the trailer remained across the third and fourth lane of our carriageway. Because of the poor visibility, three other cars had ploughed into the overturned trailer. A van that had attempted to evade everything had lost control and taken an excursion into the scenery, down an embankment.

The collision occurred at a location on the motorway that has long had a problem with standing water after heavy rain, so it was no surprise that it had happened here.

My mate and I slipped into a well-rehearsed routine, checking vehicles for drivers, passengers, and the injured. The ambulance crew was already working on the driver of one car that had collided with the lorry trailer. A few minutes later, two more ambulances, three fire tenders, and the rescue tender arrived in quick succession. From my point of view, all we could do was lend a hand where we could and let the other services do what they needed to do. The traffic was going nowhere.

I called to my mate and said that I was going to sit in the car and write up the collision, having noted vehicle types and registration marks. I envisaged we would be there for a long time. Highways had already started to move the trapped traffic off the motorway at junction 16.

As is customary, it wasn't long before the fire brigade had arranged for refreshments to be brought to the scene, and some recovery vehicles had arrived. A light rain had begun again, so my best place was writing in the car. The only lighting we had to rely on was from the fire tenders' portable lights and our spot lamps and headlamps.

I sat in the car and started writing my report when there was a knock on the passenger side window.

Nikki

I NEEDED to see Dad before I left home because I was still in bed when he left for work earlier, and I wanted to see him before returning to university.

So now I am caught in this mess. I got out of my Mini Cooper to see if my dad had sorted it out. He must be here. Our last conversation before we went to bed last night was that he was the main motorway cover today.

I wandered among the emergency vehicles. Nobody seemed to notice me; they were all busy speaking to other drivers.

'Ah, there he is.' I spotted Dad sitting in the Range Rover, with his head down, writing.

I knocked on the passenger side window. Dad looked towards the window and saw me, followed by a broad grin. He beckoned for me to get into the car. He leaned across from the driver's side and opened the door from the inside, pushing it wide open so I could get in.

'Well,' he said, 'this is a turn-up for the books. Didn't expect to see you here.'

'No, me neither, but I was still in bed when you left for work.'

'Mmmm, you caught up in all this mess, then?'

'Yeah, so it seems.'

'Is your car far away?'

'No, not too far,' I said.

'Okay, you stay here instead of standing out in that rain. What were you doing out there, anyway?'

'I thought you might be here, so I came looking for you.'

'Okay - hey, do you want a cuppa?'

'That'd be a good idea, but where will you get it from?'

'Ah, secret,' he said, tapping the side of his nose. 'See that fire truck up there?'

'Yes.'

'Well, it's really a canteen wagon – any protracted incident, the bucket boys like to get their priorities right.'

'I thought you were just joking when you've said that in the past.'

'Oh, no, now you see I wasn't!'

With a smile on his face, he got out. 'Hang on here. What do you want, tea or coffee? No, on second thoughts, I'll bring you a coffee. The tea is, well, monkey pee comes to mind.'

I laughed. 'Coffee's fine. Lots of sugar!' I shouted at him as he walked towards the fire tender. He raised his arm in acknowledgement.

A few minutes later, he returned with a hot cup of steaming coffee.

'Thanks Dad, you not having one?'

'No, got to regulate my intake. Few places to pee around here, you know.'

I giggled. 'I'd never have known you knew such language, Dad,' I said in mock disbelief.

'Well, I keep a tight rein on it when I am at home, you know; don't want the kids to get into bad ways now, do we?' he said sarcastically.

'Dad, I'm twenty-one years old. I've been at uni for twelve months. I think I know a thing or two about bad ways.'

'Yes, I am certain you do.' He looked across at me over the top of his glasses in a comedic but almost disapproving manner. We both sat in silence for a short time while he completed his collision reports.

The rain started pounding on the patrol car's roof again like jungle drums. I watched as more portable lights were put up so they could see what they needed to do, taking measurements and photographs.

A few minutes later, there was the double *whoop whoop* of another police car escorting the heavy recovery vehicle. This vehicle was big enough to put the lorry's trailer back on its wheels.

'Hang on here, love, while I talk to these guys.'

'Okay.' I snuggled down into the passenger seat and made myself comfortable. I still hadn't touched the coffee Dad had brought me.

Fifteen minutes later, Dad got back into the car.

'You okay?' he said.

'Yeah, cold, that's all.'

Dad racked up the heater in the car. 'There you are,' he said, 'that'll soon warm you up.'

'You know, Dad, you never speak about what you do at work to any of us, do you?'

He looked over at me. I was sitting low in the passenger seat, with my knees up against the dashboard. I was tall enough to do this easily. A trick I learned from the old man!

'I've never liked to burden everyone with the crap I get to see every day.'

'Surely, not every day?'

'Pretty much, if it's not some idiot who thinks he's Fangio ...'

'Who?' she exclaimed.

'Okay, Lewis Hamilton, then.'

'Ah.' The reference to high-speed drivers dawned on me.

'Or,' he continued, 'someone trying to jump off a bridge in front of a 44-tonne artic, nicking a doughnut from the services, or even watching the world go by. That is the way I spend my days. Ninety-eight per cent boredom and two per cent sheer terror!'

'But there must be lots of days when things like this don't happen?' I continued to quiz him.

'Of course, there are, but can you imagine me getting home and saying it day after day and you saying "What happened today then?" and I say something like "nothing" or "nothing exciting"? You'd think I'd got a boring job. So, I say nothing and keep you all in suspense. Then, when something like this happens, it is more exciting for you to listen to, isn't it?'

'But you always say that nothing has happened.'

'Well, there you are then; my point entirely.'

We laughed.

'But Dad, you need to tell us, let go of some of that stress you've got – a trouble shared and all that.'

'Don't you go trying out your psychoanalysis on me, young lady. I know what you're doing and what you're doing at uni, cos I'm paying for it.'

'You know I'm right, though.'

'Yes, Nikki, I know, but it is difficult sometimes.'

There was a brief silence before I said, 'I'm proud of the fact that you're a copper and that you do what you do.'

Dad looked over at me as I stared out of the window, which, by this time, was misting up a little. The demister went on.

'You know, I always got teased at school because you did what you did. They're probably all crims now for all I know, so I used to deny it – told them you worked in a factory. Whether they believed me, I don't know. And I don't know where they got the information from that you were, but I am sorry I did that. Sorry I didn't stand up for you.'

Dad had stopped writing and sat back in the driver's seat, silently watching me. I continued while staring out of the windscreen. It was as if I needed to unburden myself for something he did not know I was carrying. Dad didn't interrupt me, so I carried on.

'I think, looking back, I can say that you have done us all proud. We're all straight; none of us have gone off the rails, so to speak. Yes, you were occasionally severe with us, but we usually deserved it.'

'Mmmm, you certainly did,' Dad interjected

I nodded an acknowledgement and carried on.

'And, it's not very often we get to be alone like this, just you and me, like we used to.'

'And, pray tell where all this is leading.'

'Well, got to make the most of it. I'm going away, you know.' I looked sternly at him.

'Yes, love, but it's only up the road.'

'Right, sorry, I'm just being sentimental, but Dad, you know I love you; we all love you very much.'

I leaned over and took his hand. My hands were icy, and I'm sure he noticed. I kissed it gently.

Dad stared at me. I could see a quizzical look on his face. I knew he thought there was something wrong. Then he put his hand on mine and said, 'Look, if you have something to tell me ...'

'No.'

'You're pregnant?'

'No.'

'Getting married?'

'No.'

'God, you burnt the house down before you left?'

I giggled. He could be so dramatic sometimes. 'Noooo. I just haven't told you that in a long time. So I thought I would take the opportunity.'

In the time that Dad and I had been in conversation, the noise of the lorry trailer, as it fell back onto its wheels, made us look up. Dad's crewmate was walking towards the car.

'Don't you go away. I need to understand this a little more,' he said, shaking his head. He got out and went to talk to Mark, whom I'd met a long time ago.

They had a highly animated conversation, and both ran towards the lorry. I got out of the police car and stood by the passenger door, watching my dad.

Dave

I RAN towards the now upright trailer. Mark had told me they had found something that I needed to see. When I got to the trailer, I saw that a vehicle had been crushed under it when it had been overturned in the collision.

I stopped in my tracks, my heart pounding in my chest, and I began to sweat. I couldn't believe what I saw; the vehicle was a Mini Cooper.

It froze me to the spot. I needed to move closer to the

vehicle. The recovery men and firefighters were trying to move a tarpaulin over the vehicle to preserve the inside from the rain.

'WAIT!' I shouted, forcing myself to go to the driver's side. I looked in. The vehicle was a mangled wreck. Looking at the driver, I saw it was my beautiful daughter, Nikki.

I looked at my patrol car and saw Nikki standing next to it. She blew me a kiss, turned, and faded away. I dropped to my knees and wept.

3

A DEATH AT MIDNIGHT
PRIMUM NON NOCERE

There was always a problem getting cover for a night shift. Nobody in this day and age felt that working nights was anything other than bad for your health, except the few that took advantage of the silent hours to get away with doing, well, not a lot.

My story starts with the overnight service for a health provider that covers local doctors outside regular surgery hours. But I am not that doctor. All I do is drive them to patients' houses, but more on that later.

The overnight doctor on shift on this occasion would never be that productive. He may answer a few telephone calls but spends most of his time with his feet up on the desk and scrolling on his phone.

The attending nurse, however, was forced - reluctantly –to work her arse off to cover for him. This doctor wasn't that bothered. He only worried about how much extra he would be paid for the overnight shift. To you or me, working as a driver on a minimum wage, one hundred and seventy-five pounds an hour for doing bugger all was a bit of a stretch.

When his work was audited, he was told to pull his finger out of his backside and engage with the rest of the team, but he would not do that. If they sacked him, he would only go to another service and start again. There were plenty to choose from.

Tonight, however, was different. It was an unusually busy night. A week of appalling weather was usually enough to make the punters wonder what to do with themselves. So, contacting a service to attend to medical needs they'd probably had for weeks had become the go-to sport of the year.

The good thing was that along with this lazy doctor were three other clinicians who gave the service their all every time they came in to work.

This lazy doctor – I'm going to call him John, not his real name - had seen several patients booked in by the booking clerk. He wasn't happy about that, so he told her not to book any more for him as he was busy and to book them in with the other clinicians.

She hadn't listened to him and promptly scheduled another patient to see him. Later, she told me she was 'determined to make the bastard work for his money'!

The events that occurred before my involvement are documented, so I will relate them to you as if I were there. A fly on the wall.

THERE WAS a knock on John's consulting room door.

'Yes!' he called curtly.

A nurse entered.

'What do you want? Can't you see I'm busy?'

'Just some advice really, re a patient I'm with and you triaged on the phone.'

'Is it not something you can ask another doctor?' he snapped.

'I could, but I was told that the other doctors were engaged with patients and in any case, you triaged this patient for a face-to-face, so really, you need to see her anyway.'

'Just read my notes and get on with it. I'm too busy.'

'Yeah,' she snarled, eyeing the doctor's feet on the desk. 'I can see.'

She exhaled loudly and turned to leave. Fed up with having to put up with the same attitude from the doctor, she turned and said, 'I've been working in this service for nearly thirty years and in all that time, I've never met a doctor like you. You are arrogant and lazy and treat all the other staff like idiots. If you dismiss our service or your Hippocratic oath, I suggest you return to wherever you came from. We don't like shirkers in this environment, and I will report this attitude. Again.'

'I think you'll find I do my fair share of work.'

'You do bugger all. You arrive, secrete yourself in here, and we never hear or see you for the entire shift. You're a bloody liability to the service, and it's unfair.'

The doctor finally took his feet from the desk, put his phone down and stood up. He took a step over to the nurse.

'If you speak to me in that tone again, I will ensure you will never work as a nurse again. You are just a nurse. I am the doctor. You will not address me in that way. I am your superior. Now. Get out of my sight.'

The nurse felt arguing with him was not in her best interest. She'd tried before, and it always ended badly for her. Turning on her heel, she left the consulting room. She would, however, ensure that it would be the last time he spoke with her in those tones.

The doctor sat down, smiled, and picked up his phone.

AT TEN MINUTES TO MIDNIGHT, the booking clerk accepted into the surgery a patient whose appointment had been made for them to see a doctor. The clerk had not seen or heard from the doctor for at least an hour. He had made no telephone calls, which was nothing unusual.

It was frustrating because she also had to monitor the number of calls coming into the system. She'd reported him several times, but nothing seemed to get done. So now she'd given up. She wished he would piss off somewhere else to work.

She sent him a system message that his patient had arrived, but she got no response. Frustrated, she left the nurses' station and went to his consulting room. She knocked on the door, but there was no response. She knocked again. Nothing. Well, she would have to go in, and she'd probably find him asleep.

When she opened the door, the lights were off, but they came on as soon as she entered the room. She made as much noise as possible to wake him up, kicking his chair so it scraped the floor.

He was lying on the consulting room bed. Asleep, arms down by his sides. The clerk noticed saliva dribbling from the side of his mouth. His head was turned towards her. Then she noticed he wasn't breathing. She hit the crash button on the wall, and the other clinicians rushed into the room. Emergency resuscitation began. They tried using the defibrillator and performing CPR, but it had no effect. The doctor was pronounced dead shortly after midnight.

THIS IS where I officially come in. I work for the nighttime service as the driver of emergency vehicles, which are used to visit patients at home who cannot get to the surgery.

I'm a retired police detective whose name is, well, that's unimportant. I only do this job to keep my hand in as an advanced driver. We drive a big red Skoda Iniaq, fully liveried as a response vehicle with blue and green lights on the roof, because we also help the ambulance service when they are at full capacity.

The job can be hectic, but the night shift not so much. The drivers have room to themselves, away from anything that goes on in the surgery.

On a night shift, two of us cover half the county each. It's good because, on a night shift, I can usually get on with writing my memoirs, well, other than watching Netflix on my laptop!

Around midnight, the booking clerk burst into the driver's room. 'He's dead,' was the first thing she said to us.

'Who's dead?' I asked.

'The doctor. I've just found him in his consulting room. We've done CPR on him.' She shook her head.

'What do you want me to do?' I said.

'You were a copper! We need to know what to do next. It's not something that happens here every day, y'know.'

Like in the old job, the mechanisms I'd used for countless such jobs kicked in.

'Where is everyone now?'

'Still in there with him.'

'Let's get them all out of there then and close the door. Nobody enters the room till the police arrive. You *have* called the police?'

'Yes, the nurse has.'

'How long ago?'

'About five minutes after the other doctor pronounced death.'

'Right then, as it's unexpected, we need to let the police take the lead, okay?'

She nodded. And we left the driver's room. I went into the surgery. All the other clinical staff had now assembled in the nurses' station.

'Has the door to the consulting room been closed?' There were nods all around.

'Have any of you removed anything from the room?'

The emergency doctor said everything had been left as it was, as per protocols.

I nodded my agreement and entered the corridor with all the consulting rooms. All the doors were open except for one, which I opened.

The doctor was indeed lying on the bed. His shirt was open, and the pads for the defibrillator were still attached to him.

Apart from the detritus of the attempt to revive him, the room looked normal. A standard doctor's consulting room most likely looks like every other doctor's consulting room in the country.

The doctor's phone was on his desk, upside down. A shoe was missing from his body, which was found under his desk. A mug was on the floor beside the couch. The resuscitation team had likely pushed it over, but only a tiny amount of the content had been spilt.

I inspected the dead doctor—no apparent signs of trauma. No knives or anything sticking out of him - considering how unpopular he was, I wouldn't have been surprised if there were —no blood stains on him or his clothing.

In that case, it seemed like it may have been natural causes, but for the residue of dried saliva around his mouth. I took a step closer and inhaled. Almonds. No. That can't be right. Almonds have a recognisable smell known throughout the world, thanks to crime writers who kill their victims with cyanide.

Murder by poison was an unusual choice made popular in Agatha Christie's novels of the early twentieth century, but this was to become one of the strangest cases I had ever dealt with. I took out my phone and dialled a number I knew by heart.

Detective Chief Inspector Fletcher Randall answered the phone. He sounded as if he'd been asleep. Well, it was 1.00 am. But I knew him of old and he wasn't a heavy sleeper.

'Did I wake you?' I asked.

'No, not really. I had to get up to answer the phone cuz some silly bugger was ringing it.'

I chuckled. 'The old ones are still the old ones, Fletch.'

'Why are you ringing me at 1.30 in the effin morning?'

'I've got a suspicious death.'

'Really? I thought you'd retired.' A pause. 'Oh, you are; I remember now, I went to your retirement do.'

'Well, at the moment, it doesn't seem as if I have.'

'What's up, then?'

'It's the place where I work part-time.'

'And you have a death in a doctor's surgery? Which can't be that unusual.'

'It is when it's the doctor.'

'Oh - different.'

'They asked me to sort it out because of my background, but it's not within my purview anymore.'

'Tell me more.'

'At first, I thought it was a sudden death, with no circumstances. But when I checked the scene and the body, something was out, and there was a distinct smell of almonds on the expired breath of the corpse.'

'Almonds. Cyanide, you mean?'

'Possible, yes. I questioned it myself, but defo.'

'Okay, I'll get the ball rolling. You wanna stay there, stay involved?'

'Ha. Is the pope Catholic?'

'Yeah, that's what I thought. Where are you?'

I told Randall I was at the Emergency Care Centre in the middle of town. He hung up.

I exited the room, shut the door, and locked it. A few minutes later, two uniformed officers I knew turned up. I explained what had happened and that I'd already contacted DCI Randall, who was en route.

I RECENTLY RETIRED JUST a few months ago. Everyone on the force still knew who I was. Some didn't think I'd retired. They also couldn't understand why a retired detective inspector would want to work at all. To cut a long story short, I put it down to institutionalisation. The same as prisoners who only knew what life was like in prison and couldn't cope with life outside.

It's not as bad as that, but the principle is the same. I'd spoken to retired cops who'd been out of the job for ten or twenty years, who still felt lost without that camaraderie and esprit de corps.

But here I was, embroiled in another suspicious death. Something I thought I'd left behind.

I was standing in the corridor to the consulting rooms. A police officer had stationed himself outside the room with the victim still inside. Randall had been in and viewed the deceased. The manner and cause of his death perplexed both him and me.

'Seems a strange way to go,' I said.

Randall nodded. 'Yes, and he had been in the room alone during the shift.'

'Apart from the times he saw patients, of course.'

Randall nodded again. 'Nobody took him a drink?'

'Not that I've ascertained.'

'Well, I suppose we'd better talk to everyone here.'

'You'd better, yes.'

'What about you?'

'Well, I was in the building. I'm happy to help where I can, but I'm not a cop anymore, remember.'

'Right.' He laughed. 'You've heard of the saying "once a copper, always a copper"?'

'I've heard!'

THE SURGERY HAD BEEN CLOSED, and the senior on-call management team for the service had turned up. They seemed supportive of what was happening, but you couldn't tell.

The executive director of the service, a man of about six feet, with greying and receding hair, grey eyes and about 50 years old, had arrived some fifteen minutes ago. He need not have bothered – there was nothing he could do other than stick his nose where Randall certainly didn't want it.

We were all gathered in the communications room, a windowless, claustrophobic space with grey walls and an enormous TV screen at one end with rows of numbers identifying the number of calls waiting, dropped and answered.

'Thank you all for waiting,' Randall said.

'Didn't have much choice, did we?' my driver colleague said —a grumpy old bugger at the best of times. Randall acknowledged him with a curt nod.

'As you are aware, one of your colleagues died tonight in circumstances that are suspicious, and we are treating this event as a homicide.'

'You think one of us killed him?' the senior nurse exclaimed. 'We tried to resuscitate him!'

'I understand that, but we need to keep all options open until we know more. I'm going to ask my retired colleague, Paul, to assist me as my eyes and ears on the ground, so to speak. At some point, we will need formal statements from all of you about your activities this evening.

'For now, I need to know where you all were at the material time. As you seemed eager to get off, let's start with you.' He pointed at my driver colleague.

'I was in the drivers' room next door all evening, apart from when I checked the car earlier. Apart from that, I never moved out of the room. I was with Paul all evening.'

Randall looked over at me. I nodded.

After the initial interviews, I walked out of the surgery with Randall.

'Well, what do you think?' I asked. 'First impressions?'

'I'm not entirely convinced everyone was telling me the truth.'

'A couple of them seemed fairly vague about their whereabouts. It's not rocket science; they were either in their rooms or weren't.'

'Any CCTV inside?'

'No, only outside. There's one opposite the main door to the surgery and a few others dotted around the site.'

'At least we can get a timeline of who came and went with the one on the door.'

'I'll see if I can get my hands on it later.'

We'd got back to Randall's car. The dawn was breaking. There was a sliver of silver-grey light forcing its way through the clouds.

'Sorry we had to meet up like this,' I said.

'Don't worry. It was always meant to be,' Randall said.

'Remember what I said earlier about always being a copper.' He blipped the lock on his car and jumped in. 'I'll give you an update later.'

He started the car and drove away.

~

A FEW DAYS LATER, I met Randall in the old coffee shop opposite the nick. The scenes-of-crime team had thoroughly investigated the scene in the preceding two days, gathering evidence, bagging it, and forwarding it to the laboratory. I'd been there for those days, helping where I could.

We'd sat at a table at the rear of the coffee shop, away from listening ears.

'What have we got then, Fletch?'

'A bit of a conundrum, really, Paul.'

'In what way?'

'The PM results show a different story to what we thought happened.'

'And?'

'According to the evidence from your staff who tried to resuscitate the doctor, they pronounced death two minutes past midnight.'

'That would seem about right.'

'The pathologist, however, puts the time of death between eight and eleven PM.'

'Yes, but you know as well as I do that's always a bit of a guesstimate.'

'You can see it puts a different light on things?'

'We were swamped that night. Unusually so. That doctor wasn't well-liked. He was arrogant and thought himself a cut above the rest.'

'Yes, I'd heard that from more than one of those I

interviewed on the night. The senior nurse had a row with him about some advice she needed.'

'So, she could be in the frame then?'

'Possibly. I need to check the time of this altercation with him.'

I took a gulp of my coffee and looked around the cafe. There were more coppers in there than members of the public. I recognised a few faces, both good and bad, in my experience.

'What else have you got?'

'The problem is the amount of DNA, which may not lead us anywhere because of the number of people who use the room.'

'But the clinical staff wipe all the rooms down with antiseptic wipes before seeing patients.'

'Right. That's good to know, but we'll have to see.'

'Anything else you need?'

Randall looked around and lowered his voice before putting his mug down. He'd been warming his hands on it. 'Can you get into the records of those patients who attended so we can do some background checks? If the time of death was between eight and eleven, it also puts all who saw him in prime position.'

'Can't be done, I'm afraid. I'm not even allowed to access my own records, let alone a patient's unless it's because of them calling us.'

'We could get a warrant?'

'Doubt it will get you very far; the health service is extremely protective about its data - for obvious reasons.'

'Okay, not to worry. We'll have to do it the old-fashioned way.'

'Ah. But I *can* get you the names of the patients between those times. At least you can check PNC and local intelligence.'

'Good point. Let me know when you've got them.'

'I'll ping them across to you.'

~

A FURTHER WEEK PASSED. The initial rush to get things done in quick time had slowed to something more manageable. Randall had kept me apprised daily. He didn't need to do that, but I suppose it came down to professional courtesy, even though I was retired. We got on well together when we were both DIs, so it was good of him to do that.

Randall called me early Friday morning. When I arrived, he invited me into the office, which was a hive of activity.

Meeting me in the foyer of MIT, he said, 'I think we know who the killer is.'

'Good news, then.'

'Good news, indeed.'

I walked into my old office. Nothing had changed—the old crew with a smattering of new ones. The older faces coming out with jibes about being unable to stay away. I'd heard and given them all before.

The murder board timeline was new. I'd had to occasionally wheel in an old whiteboard from the training room to make mine up.

Randall showed me it was interactive and connected to HOLMES. Transfer of data from there to the board was as easy as blinking. No scrawling with whiteboard pens that kept running out.

'What's our timeline?' I asked.

'Okay, so what we know is at 20:00, our victim arrives at the centre. The booking clerk and the nurse he later argued with meet him.

'According to the booking clerk, he went to his consulting room. He saw a few patients at 20:35, 21:15 and 22:00. We know from the data supplied by the service that he was talking with patients on the telephone at 20:15, 20:50 and 21:00. After that, he made no further calls.'

'That's slap bang in the middle of what the pathologist said was the time of death.'

'Correct. Interesting, yes?'

I nodded for him to continue.

'He contacted the last patient he saw at 22:00. Known to us for mental health issues. There is no evidence to suggest that she had any hand in his death.'

'So, if the other clinicians were where they say they were, how did he get cyanide administered to him?' I asked.

Randall looked at me and smiled. 'But they weren't where they say they were.'

'Ah. Tell me more.'

'You told me your other driver never left the driver's room.'

I nodded. 'He may have left to go to the loo or something, make coffee, et cetera, but he was around, shall we say.'

'We have him on CCTV outside with his car at about 22:15.'

'Right, yes, I remember now. There was talk of a patient visit that got cancelled around that time. So where was he?'

Randall directed me to his computer and showed me the CCTV feed. I saw the driver searching through the car. He opens the boot, recovers something from the back, and puts it in his pocket. I couldn't see what he had taken.

'What's he had away from the car?'

'Codeine sulphate. It turns out he has an addiction to painkillers, but watch on.'

The driver was leaning against the car when the second, younger nurse from the centre came out and joined him. They walked off together, out of sight of the camera, coming back into view some twenty minutes later.

'Well, I'll be ...'

'Yes, he admitted in another interview that he and the nurse - both married - were having a relationship.'

'Shagging, then?'

Randall laughed. 'You could say that, yes. But that only takes them out of the frame for what, thirty to forty minutes at the most.'

'Correct, but what do you know about the other doctor on duty?'

'Nice enough guy. Diligent. Works well but prefers to be out in the car, racing around the countryside.'

'It turns out he has form.'

'Really?'

'A few years ago, he was working in London when a patient he was administering to, following an RTC, died because he gave a huge dose of ketamine and fentanyl. He nearly got struck off. He went into general practice and moved up here.'

'He's a partner at one surgery, I think.'

'Indeed, and well respected, we've discovered. But on the night in question, he and our deceased were in the kitchen. Not arranged, just happened. We tested the mug we found in the consulting room, and a residue of sodium nitroprusside – a cyanogenic - was found in it. We believe he brought it to work intending to do away with our victim.'

'Why? Do we know?'

'Not at the moment, but we have him in custody. You want to watch?'

I nodded eagerly. This was a revelation and totally unexpected for this doctor.

~

THE OBSERVATION ROOM in the interview suite hadn't changed at all. There were some new flat-screen monitors, but that was about it. Some wag had put an old World War Two poster about walls having ears on the wall.

I sat down with a young DC I didn't know. I introduced myself, as did he. He said little. He was unsure why a retired DI was sitting with him.

Just as Randall entered the room, he offered me headphones, which I took and placed on my head. The doctor, in a standard-issue grey tracksuit, was sitting against the wall in the corner. His solicitor was beside him, with a tablet ready to make notes.

Randall had a file in front of him he'd put on the desk. There was probably nothing of importance in it. It was there for show. I know; I'd done it myself in the past. The last thing I hoped he wasn't going for was a "no comment" interview.

After the interview formalities were over, Randall started with one sentence that would hopefully encourage the doctor to talk.

'Doctor, we are here today to allow you to talk about how and why you killed your colleague, to clear up anything we may have misunderstood.'

The doctor stared at Randall. No emotion. Blank faced. Resigned. It was at least a minute before he finally spoke.

'I will confess to the mercy killing of my colleague.'

'Mercy killing?'

The doctor nodded. 'It's a long story?'

'We have plenty of time.'

'Very well. Ten years ago, when he arrived in the UK, I took him under my wing in our surgery. He was young and unacquainted with how we did things in the health service. He was initially attentive and worked well with other colleagues.

'The problem was his holier-than-thou character, and we

saw his true colours after some time. He was obsessed with money. Working all hours he could. He turned against the nurses, and the day he assaulted my wife, knocking her unconscious, and who now suffers from epilepsy, was the day we let him go.'

'What happened, then?' Randall asked.

'We hoped he would just go back to his own country.'

'But he didn't?'

The doctor shook his head.

'How long have you been working in the emergency doctor service?'

'I started after we let him go, and it was all good. We're a good team and work well together. We gelled as a team should. We knew each other's strengths and weaknesses.'

'But?'

The doctor stared around the stark interview room. His face was still blank - unemotional. Only coming to the fore when he spoke about his wife.

'Did you have any thoughts about killing him?'

'No, not at all. It's not in my nature.'

'Clearly, it is; otherwise, you would have thought of another method to resolve your issues with him. Humans all have the potential to kill. It's in our nature, neanderthal almost. You, of all people, should know that.'

'That depends on your upbringing - nature or nurture they call it, if I remember my psychology classes. By nature, I'm not a psychopathic killer.'

'What are you, then?'

The doctor shrugged. 'An opportunist, probably.'

Randall shook his head. 'You saw an opportunity to get your own back for injuring your wife. Is that what you're telling me?'

'Seems that way, yes.'

'When did you decide to kill him?'

'When he was in the kitchen with me.'

'Why?'

'He came in, in that arrogant way he has, complaining about a patient he'd just seen. She's what we call a frequent flyer.'

'She's seen as a burden on the service?'

'I wouldn't say she was a burden, just that she can't access the service she needs.' The doctor rubbed his face, tiredness beginning to show.

'What did he say about her?'

'He said she needed a good seeing to sort her head out.'

'Meaning?'

'She's a pretty young female. He probably wanted to fuck her.'

'Had he said anything like this before?'

'God, yes. The sort of person who'd screw anything in a skirt. Sees it as his right.'

Randall said nothing.

The doctor continued, 'I got fed up with him and his ways. He hadn't changed in the time he'd been off my radar. Still arrogant and misogynistic.'

'So you put him down?'

'You could say that.'

'Where did you get the cyanide from?'

'In emergency medicine, sodium nitroprusside is used to rapidly decrease blood pressure. But if you give too much, well, the consequences are fatal.'

'And that's what you did?'

The doctor nodded. 'I had a vial in my possession and poured it into his coffee cup when he wasn't looking.'

'Did you expect him to die?'

He nodded. 'I suppose I did, yes.'

'What did you do when you went to resuscitate him?'

'Only went through the motions. I did as little as possible, just enough for the others to think I was trying my best.'

'Why did you want to be a doctor?'

'Like all who join the profession. To help people.'

'I don't understand why you deliberately, with malice aforethought, killed a colleague?'

'He was nothing. He was never a doctor because his moral compass pointed in the opposite direction to everyone else's.'

'As is yours,' Randall remarked.

The doctor shrugged. 'No comment.'

Randall removed a sheet of paper from his file and showed it to the doctor.

'Do you recognise this?'

He leaned forward and nodded.

'Is that your signature at the bottom?'

He nodded again.

'Can you read the paragraph I've marked.'

The doctor picked up the sheet of paper and read out loud. '*I will help the sick, and I will abstain from all intentional wrongdoing and harm.*'

'Primum non nocere,' Randall said. 'First, do no harm!'

'I'm fully aware of that, Inspector.'

'And how do you feel, not abiding by that oath?'

'How do you think I feel?'

'I don't know till you tell me.'

The doctor looked away, not saying anything.

'Are you glad he's dead?'

'I am, yes. And I'd do the same thing again under the same circumstances.'

'You have no shame, no remorse. You are no better than the man you killed in cold blood. Just as arrogant. I certainly see a cold-hearted killer before me, not a warm-hearted healer. You'll be charged with murder, doctor. Interview suspended, 22:45hrs.'

Randall instructed an officer to escort the doctor back to his cell and met me coming out of the observation room. I was disappointed with the doctor, whom I considered a friend. We'd worked together many times. But hearing what he said in his interview shed a new light on him and sent my blood cold. How can anyone hide such a personality from others? His secret ability to even consider taking a life without a thought for his Hippocratic oath. His admission in interviews could only mean that he'd get a lifelong prison sentence.

A FEW WEEKS after all this, I had returned to being a retired copper when I got a call from Randall.

'Paul, how's things?' Randall asked.

'All good here, mate. What's the next murder you want me to solve?' I chuckled.

'I'll let you know, but I thought I'd tell you about your doctor friend.'

'And?'

'He's dead. Committed suicide in his cell, yesterday.'

4

THE COVER UP

In October 1986, a young detective constable, Brent Fortune, was on patrol in the Midlands town of Ashlinghurst when he was called to the scene of a burglary at a large house in a well-to-do area. When he arrived, two officers were already at the scene, waiting outside. He approached them and, after the usual greetings, said, 'What have we got, then?'

The older of the two officers replied, 'Got a suspicious death inside. Male. Early forties. Naked. Bottom of the stairs.'

'I thought this was a burglary?' Fortune said.

'So did we,' the older officer replied.

'Fell or pushed?' Fortune said.

'Well, there ain't anyone else in the 'ouse,' the second younger officer commented, clearly irritated by something.

'Okay, show me,' he said to the older officer, and told the younger officer to stay put. As they walked into the house, Fortune said, 'What's blowing up your mate's skirt, then?'

The officer grunted. 'Shoulda finished an hour ago, that's what.'

'Sorry I couldn't get here any earlier,' Fortune replied with more than a bit of sarcasm.

They entered the hallway of the house, which was moderately furnished. Minimalist, with white painted walls. No pictures. In reality, Fortune thought, quite stark. Clinical almost.

'Is he the only occupant and owner?' Fortune asked.

'At the moment, we're assuming it's him,' pointing to the dead man at the bottom of the stairs. Naked. As described. Spread eagled with his left leg resting on the bottom step.

There was blood around the victim's head, which had seeped into the hallway carpet, turning the white carpet into a gross shade of pink. There also appeared to be another injury underneath the man, but they couldn't confirm that until SOCO arrived.

'No sign how this happened?'

'Nothing we've discovered thus far.'

'How did we get the call?'

'The brother of the victim arrived at the house to find him like this.'

'What time?'

''Bout 6.30 pm.'

'Where is he now?'

'He's gone.'

'Really?' Fortune sounded surprised.

'Said he couldn't stand to see him like that. Which I suppose is plausible.'

'But he should have stayed. Why did you let him leave?'

'Had little choice in the matter.'

'Why?'

'Duty Inspector got his details then told him to fuck off.'

'Great, I better ring the on-call Homicide Response.'

'Control room has already done that.'

'Saves me a job, then. Let's go. Secure the scene.'

IN APRIL 2008, the young detective who investigated his first murder in 1986 was now a detective chief superintendent and closing in on retirement.

Brent Fortune had spent his service in CID, but that first case back in 1986 had always bugged him. It remained undetected, and the matter of how Logan Chalk, aka Peter Le Pierre, came to be at the bottom of the stairs had always been up for debate. It would be the icing on the cake if he could detect it before he retired. For now, he had to put it to one side, like the past thirty-two years, and get on with the list of the day's work. To cap it all, he was also the on-call Silver Commander that night. He didn't mind when he wasn't called out, but that seemed to be few and far between these last few months.

At about seven, he got home to his wife, showered, changed into something a little more comfortable, and sat down for dinner with his wife, Monica, and a glass of wine. The rest of the evening was uneventful, and at 10:30 p.m., he retired to bed.

HIS PHONE WOKE him at 2.22 am. Groggily, he answered it.

'Yes.' He coughed to clear his throat.

'Sorry to wake you, sir,' the control room inspector said, 'but we have a situation.'

'That being?'

'We're at the scene of a murder in Barton-on-the-Nene, looks like a home invasion.'

'Any decedents?'

'One. Male. Mid to late sixties. And naked.'

That comment woke Brent up. 'What's the address?'

The inspector reeled off the address. 'Okay, I'll be there in twenty.'

Brent hung up, dressed, and told his wife where he was going before putting coffee into a travel mug and jumping into his F-Pace Jaguar. As the senior on-call officer, he had it fitted with covert blue lights, so he powered off the drive with everything on.

Twenty-five minutes later, Brent landed at the address in Barton-on-the-Nene.

Detective Inspector Harry Pollard greeted him and briefed him about the scene.

Now attired in his white SOCO suit, he entered the small 1950s bungalow, where he saw the body of a man face down on the kitchen floor and lying in a pool of blood.

Strangely, the victim's left leg was resting on a portable step, and clearly, there were other injuries on the body.

'We think he may have fallen off the stool,' Pollard said.

'Why would he be standing on a stool naked?'

'Wanted to get something from the cupboard. Couldn't sleep or whatever,' Pollard said.

'Possible,' Brent said, 'but I think improbable.'

'Why?'

'I've seen this before, and I feel that this one will not be easy, Harry.'

'MO?'

Brent nodded. 'If we can turn him over, I'll know.'

The senior SOCO and another obliged after photographs were taken of the victim in situ. They turned the body over.

Harry gasped. He wasn't ready for what he saw. Etched into the chest of the man was the word "BITCH". The reason for so much blood was evident to Harry and Brent. The killer had removed the man's genitals.

'Fucking hell,' Harry exclaimed.

'Indeed, Harry. And yes. This is a copycat or the same person we never caught at the first murder I ever went to as a junior detective.'

'I remember something about that. What was his name?'

'Peter Le Pierre, aka Logan Chalk'

'Parents had a sense of humour. Peter the Peter.' Harry chuckled. 'Do we know who this man is?'

'I recognise the face. This is retired Superintendent Dan Metcalf. He was the duty inspector at that 1986 murder. He got disciplined for allowing a witness, his step-brother, to leave the crime scene after he found him. They never proved it, but they always believed there was a familial connection.'

'Wasn't he asked about it?'

'Several times. But he kept schtum.'

'Any ideas who did it back then?'

'There were rumours but no evidence to prove it. All lines of enquiry got shut down. We really did not know. No suspects.'

'What, nothing at all?'

Brent shook his head, then rubbed a hand through his hair. Pushing back the skull cap hat he was wearing.

'Whoever did this could be in the frame for the 1986 job?' Brent commented, more to himself than to Harry.

'It's time we probably re-visited that case, anyway.'

'Does he have any family?'

'I know his wife died a few years ago. Cancer. I don't think they had any children.'

'What about this brother? Sister?'

'He has a step-brother somewhere. He never mentioned him, as far as I'm aware.'

'Better get cracking, then,' Harry said, and they both left the SOCOs to it.

∼

A DAY LATER, Brent left the post-mortem with Harry.

'What would encourage anyone to cut off a man's cock and balls?' Brent said, thinking out loud.

'There must be a reason. Either ritualistic slaying or a female - woman scorned and all that.'

'Or a man, nowadays, could be pissed off at getting another partner. Some queer guy's revenge, I suppose.'

'The word BITCH on his chest, though, smacks to me of homophobia. Did the '86 guy have the same?'

Brent nodded. 'We couldn't work that out, either.'

'Well, somebody out there,' Harry said, spreading his arms wide, 'knows what happened to both of them.'

'And we need to find them PDQ,' Brent said.

The end-of-the-day briefing seemed to offer a glimmer of hope. Dan Metcalf had a relative through marriage who had already been contacted and collected from her daily tennis workout some miles away as they spoke. What was likely to be a reasonably tricky conversation was the exact opposite.

Angela Fitzherbert, the sister-in-law to the dead superintendent, was less than happy, having been gathered up while playing her game of tennis.

'Why am I here?' she demanded in a shrill upper-class accent. She was still wearing her tennis gear. For a fifty-something woman, she still had the looks, and Brent noticed the bronzed legs.

'We are investigating the murder of your brother-in-law. You appear to be his only living relative.

'I see. He was my sister's husband, but she passed away some years ago.' She crossed herself. 'Too long ago now,' she repeated quietly to herself.

'You don't seem worried about his passing,' Harry said.

Angela shot a scornful look at him.

'When was the last time you saw your brother-in-law?' Brent said.

'Not since my sister died. We don't keep in touch.'

'How long ago was that exactly?' Harry asked.

'Got to be ten years. Something like that.'

'And you've not seen him since?'

'That's what I just said, didn't I.'

'And you're not bothered?'

'Why should I? It's not as if he's kin. Bad things happen to people.'

'Harold Kushner,' Harry said.

'Sorry?'

'From Harold Kushner. "Why do bad things happen to *good* people." Was *he* good?'

Angela looked nonplussed. 'An educated cop. That's a first.'

'Was he good?' Harry pressed.

'Not a man I would trust, let's put it that way.'

'Why?'

'He was a copper, that's why. Wouldn't trust any of you as far as I could hit a tennis ball.'

'You've had an unpleasant experience with us?' Harry said.

Angela guffawed. 'No shit, Sherlock.'

Brent said, 'Let's get back to it, shall we?'

Angela moved to sit down but remained standing, putting her weight on one hip and glowering at the two officers.

'We need to identify the remains and confirm who it is. Are you able to do that?'

'Do I have a choice?'

'Not really, no,' Harry said gruffly, deciding that he didn't like this upper-class snob.

'I hope you are not expecting me to go dressed like this?'

'We can do it tomorrow. If that's okay with you.'

'I suppose it'll have to be.'

'We'll get a car to pick you up.'

'Don't bother. I'll make my own way. Can I go now?'

Harry took Angela Fitzherbert to the door.

'What a charming woman,' Harry said on his return.

'Something not right there,' Brent said.

Harry smiled. 'Probably just pissed off that we interrupted her tennis game.'

SEVERAL WEEKS PASSED, and Harry and Brent became concerned that the case would slowly get put in the freezer. Again. Brent didn't want that to happen. And then a call changed the whole dynamic of the case. He rang DI Pollard.

'You busy, Inspector?'

'Nothing that can't wait, sir.'

'Meet me at headquarters in an hour. There's somebody we need to talk to.'

The force registry is the depository for all paperwork generated by the force, past and present. In the basement below, there are significant files dating back to the formation of the County Constabulary in 1886.

Information is stored today, however, on computer discs, smart drives, and in The Cloud. Much of the paperwork left in the basement was slowly being scanned into a computer, no longer subject to the vagaries of time in a damp and dusty atmosphere. Only papers of historical significance were kept in paper form and retained by the forces' historical unit.

In 1986, though, the force had few computers. The scanning of those documents brought Brent and Harry to HQ today.

Situated in the oldest part of the manor, which was force headquarters, the fusty smell of ancient paper and years of dust hit both of them as they entered through the large oak door. Behind the facade of the ancient door was a large office with industrial printers and scanners whirring away as they walked up to reception.

'Can I help you?' A small, world-weary, bespectacled man with greying hair and facial colour to match addressed them both.

'We're looking into the 1986 death of Peter Le Pierre. Somebody wanted to speak with us,' Brent said.

'Ah, yes. Follow me, please.' The man came out from behind the reception desk in a motorised wheelchair and zoomed off down a corridor. They were ushered into a small ante-room off the main office and told to wait.

A few moments later, a portly woman, smartly dressed in a dark green trouser suit, entered the room with a pile of files in her arms. She would be in her sixties. Although grey and dyed with a pinkish hue, her hair was immaculately kept. Not a hair out of place. It looked like she'd used a whole can of hairspray to keep it in place, Brent thought.

'Good morning, gentlemen,' she said as she banged the dusty files on the table in front of them. A plume of dust rose from the table.

'As you can see,' she started with no further preamble, 'these folders were due for scanning this week, but we are aware of the two enquiries ongoing with a similar MO. So we kept the files out.'

'That was fortunate,' Brent said.

'I think so, given what I have found buried deep in the paperwork.'

'And what have you found?' Harry said.

She pulled out a chair and sat down. Brent and Harry followed suit.

'How does the 1986 enquiry fit in with the current one?' Harry said.

'Well, you'd think they wouldn't, would you? But as I scanned the documents, I noticed a pattern. It's something I do,' she said, smiling.

'A pattern?' Brent said.

'In what respect?' Harry asked.

'Peter Le Pierre, not his real name, by the way, was a predatory homosexual.' She opened the file and showed them a document from Crime Intelligence.

'Why is this report redacted?' Brent said.

'A good question, Chief Superintendent. There is, however, an unredacted copy in the file from the same source.'

She showed them the report and then explained.

'Peter got murdered in 1986 when he was in his early fifties, and according to the files, he was virtually written off because of ill health, possibly HIV, which was at its height back then.'

'Why didn't we know about this at the time?' Brent said.

She shrugged. 'Above my pay grade!' She smiled again.

'Were you here then?'

'As a junior assistant, yes.'

'And all you did is file this stuff?'

She nodded.

'So why else do you want to talk to us?' Brent asked.

She opened another file. 'This is the personal file for your retired superintendent, Daniel Metcalf. The connection is his second brother, Clayton Metcalf.'

'We didn't know he had a second brother. Fitzherbert did not mention it,' Harry said.

'He does, but I think the term *estranged* comes to mind,' the registrar said.

'So what's the connection with Peter?'

'From what I can determine through these files, Clayton is fully invested with Peter's gay goings-on.'

'So, this should be present?' Brent said.

'Correct. But it isn't. It's missing.'

'How can it be missing?'

'It's recorded as having arrived at the registry, but there is no record of it leaving.'

'Is it scanned in?'

She shook her head. 'No. It's all here.'

'What do we know about the person who last had it?'

'That would be Superintendent Metcalf, and that was the last time it was reviewed before he retired. We don't know where it's been since then.'

'Could he have removed any incriminating documentation before he retired?'

'That's the only conclusion I can come to,' she said.

'If I remember correctly, our superintendent, then an inspector, sent his brother away from the scene. And the witness statement he gave said that he'd found him like that when he visited him.'

'There was little CCTV in 1986, but the investigating officer, your boss at the time, Mr Fortune, secured a private video reel showing Clayton Metcalf in the area well before he says he was.'

'Do you think something was going on between them?'

'Yes, and I think the duty inspector knew about it.'

'And sent him away,' Brent said.

'Are we saying that Clayton murdered Peter, and now he's come back years later to finish the job?'

'Sounds as if that's the case,' Harry said.

'But why kill his brother?' Brent said.

'People will do anything to keep secrets,' Harry said.

'So it looks like you have a double murder to solve, Mr Fortune,' the registrar said.

Brent nodded. 'Get all this stuff to the incident room, and we'll look at it there.'

They thanked the registrar for bringing the information to their attention and returned to the incident room.

THE FOLLOWING DAY, a bored officer stationed at the front desk of the police station where Brent and Harry worked sat behind the desk. He'd had no visitors that day, and it was only 11.00 am – he'd got another five hours to do. And he hated desk duty because you had to deal with all the crap people brought to the police as if they had the answer to everything.

The doors slid open, and a well-dressed man in a pink polo shirt and sand-coloured chinos, with pepper-pot hair and a beard, walked towards the officer. The officer stood up.

'Yes, sir. Can I help you?'

The man stood in front of the officer and simply said, 'I'd like to confess to the murder of my brother.'

Not believing his ears, the officer said, 'Excuse me, what?'

'I believe you heard me the first time, officer.'

The officer offered the man a seat. 'Can I take your name.'

'I'm Clayton Metcalf.'

The officer had seen the daily 'wanted' sheet and knew who he was. He left the confines of the front desk, walked around to where Clayton was sitting, and told him to stand up before placing him under arrest and arranging his transportation to the central lock-up. Then, he made a telephone call upstairs.

Meanwhile, Brent and Harry were mulling over the files sent up from the registry upstairs. The phone rang in Brent's pocket. He answered it with his surname. He listened, said nothing, then cleared the call.

'Well?' questioned Harry.

Brent gave him a wide grin. 'Clayton is in lock-up.'

'How come?' Harry said.

'Just handed himself in.'

'Bloody hell,' Harry said, whipping his coat off the back of the chair. 'Let's see what he has to say for himself.'

BRENT AND HARRY logged into the custody suite at the town's central lock-up. The officer who made the arrest met them at the custody desk.

'I've had him booked in, sirs,' the officer said as he greeted them.

'I don't know you, officer. How long have you been with us?'

'Six months, sir.'

'I don't suppose you ever thought that you'd be arresting a murderer in your first few months of service, did you?'

The officer looked embarrassed. 'Actually,' he said, 'it's my very first arrest since I finished my rotations.'

'One for your family stories when you've retired, then,' Brent said with a wide grin. 'You can have the pleasure of bringing him down to Interview one.'

'Thank you, sir, I'll bring him along.'

Brent and Harry set up the interview room. After bringing

Clayton from the cells, Brent invited the young constable to observe from the gallery.

Clayton was calm and appeared resigned to his fate. He was polite and answered questions truthfully.

After confirming his name and credentials, Brent said, 'You attended our police station earlier this morning of your own free will.'

'I did, yes.'

'Are you now prepared to be interviewed without the presence of a solicitor?'

'I am, yes. I've been burdened with this for long enough.'

'Why are you here?' Harry asked.

'I wish to confess.'

'To what?'

'The deaths of my lover and my brother.'

'And they are?' Brent said.

'Peter Le Pierre, also known as Logan Chalk, and Dan Metcalf.'

Brent sat back in his chair and folded his arms. 'Why come to us now?'

'I never meant to kill Dan. That was an accident.'

'But you mutilated his body all the same.'

Clayton made no response.

'Tell me what happened in 1986, Clayton.'

Clayton sat forward, resting his arms on the table, and took a sip of water from a paper cup Harry had brought him.

Brent could see in the man's eyes that all this had taken a toll on his life.

Clayton sat back and slumped against the wall. Defeated. Then he recounted his story.

'In 1986, I was a young man still trying to find my way in the world and who I was. I realised I'm not attracted to women, but men, and concluded almost immediately that I was gay.'

'Did that upset you?' Harry asked.

'In a way, I suppose it did. I do like women; I don't have any desire to shag them. I met Logan, or should I say, Peter, as he preferred, in a club in town in early '85. He was charming, and we hit it off straight away despite being a good few years older than me.'

He took another sip of water.

'Did you move in with him?'

'No. We decided not to cohabit. We just spent a lot of time in each other's homes. He had a house. I have a flat outside town.

'In early 1986, I suspected he was seeing someone else. I was determined to find out what was happening, so I went to his house on the day I was not supposed to meet him.

'And what did you find at his house?' Harry asked.

'I was stunned. I sneaked in through the back door, for which I have a key, and went straight upstairs and into the bedroom to find him fucking his ex-wife.'

'He was bi?' Harry asked.

Clayton nodded. 'I didn't know. I'd only ever seen him with men.'

'What happened to his ex after you found them together?' Harry said.

'She quickly got dressed and left. I had an enormous row with Peter.'

'How did he get to the bottom of the stairs?' Brent asked.

'The row spilled out onto the landing. I was so angry with him, I pushed him down the stairs.'

'Was it your intention to kill him?' Harry asked.

'Probably. I never really gave it much thought.'

'Why would you mutilate Peter's body?'

'Revenge. Blind revenge for screwing me over - literally.' The briefest of smiles. For the first time, Clayton became more animated. 'I don't know how long he'd been having it off with his ex. He was being a bitch, so it was only appropriate that everyone knew, and he wasn't able to do it again to anyone.'

'What do you mean by that?' Harry asked.

'He needed to understand that you can't do that to people, so he needed to lose his manhood so he wouldn't do it again.'

'Why? He was dead at the bottom of the stairs.'

Clayton looked away.

'He was dead, wasn't he, Clayton?' Brent asked.

Clayton said nothing.

'Clayton. Answer the question, please?' Harry asked.

'No, he wasn't. He was just unconscious.'

'You could have saved him, couldn't you?'

No response.

'Couldn't you?' Brent said, raising his voice.

'I could. But I didn't. I thought he deserved it.'

'And by mutilating the body as you did, you sealed his fate to a long and agonising death.'

Clayton nodded.

'What happened when Inspector Metcalf - your brother - arrived?'

'I spoke to him and he told me to go home and that he'd make sure he wouldn't get me involved. And he was true to his word. I never got a visit from the police.'

'What about forensics at the scene?'

Clayton shrugged. 'I suppose Dan made them disappear too.'

'And what about Peter's ex?'

'She just disappeared. I've not had sight or sound of her.'

'And there was no interview, either?'

'Not that I know of?'

Brent suspended the interview to give them all a break. Clayton was taken back to his cell.

'We need to speak to the ex-wife,' Harry declared.

'Let's get that young cop to do some research for us. Give him some kudos for the arrest.'

Harry nodded, then left Brent mulling things over in his office.

Later that afternoon, a second interview took place with Clayton.

'Why did you wait so long to go after your brother?' Brent started.

'I didn't kill him. It was an accident.'

'So you say, but you staged it like Peter's death.'

Clayton didn't respond.

'Did you want us to believe that Peter's killer was once more among us?'

'The idea crossed my mind.'

'I think it did more than cross your mind. I think you set out deliberately to kill your brother because he was going to spill the beans about your involvement in Peter's murder.'

'No, that's not the case.'

'What happened in the intervening years between Peter and your brother's death?'

'I got banged up for a robbery that went wrong, and then I moved abroad and got myself banged away in a prison in Germany. I must stop meeting the wrong sort of people.' Clayton gave a wan smile.

'What decided that it was time to dispose of your brother?'

'I hadn't seen him since he got me out of Peter's murder. I thought it best to stay away. He was a copper, after all.'

'Something must have brought it back to where it all started?' Brent said.

Clayton thought for a moment before answering. 'Dan contacted me out of the blue. I didn't know he knew where I was or how to get in touch. But he is - was - senior Old Bill.

Anyway, he said that the cold case team contacted him, who were looking into Peter's death again. Dan, of course, had been retired by then for a good few years. But he told me he couldn't keep our secret anymore.'

'What did you decide to do?' Harry said. 'Was it then you killed him?'

'No. I had no intention of killing him, as I've already said. It was an accident. I just needed to speak with him.

'I went to his home late one evening. He was getting ready for bed. We went into the kitchen, and we argued about it. Obviously, I didn't want him to give the game away, but he said it had haunted him all his service, and since he retired, he needed to make peace with himself.

'I hit him. I was angry that he hadn't even thought about what it would do to me. He fell against the fridge and hit his head on the corner of the kitchen unit as he went down. Killed him outright. I'd no intention to hurt him.'

'But you mutilated his body in the same way you did to Peter. Why?' Brent said.

'I can't answer that question. Perhaps the trauma of killing Peter overtook me, and I became that person again like life repeating itself.

'I thought about it for days because I still don't know. In here.' He tapped his head and leaned forward. 'I know I'm going to prison. I accept that with the fact that I'll probably die in there. But that's okay. My life has been shit for most of it, so it may as well finish as shit.'

'Your remorse may help your sentence. That you've come voluntarily to us and have responded to our questions.'

'Maybe, but I doubt it,' Clayton said. 'I don't think I have anything else to say to you.'

Brent and Harry concluded the interview and stood. In front of the custody sergeant, Clayton was charged with the murder of Peter Le Pierre (aka Logan Chalk) and Daniel Metcalf.

Sentenced to twenty-five years, he died in prison after twenty years from medical complications following surgery.

Brent retired, happy in the knowledge that he had caught the killer of his first murder and that of his old boss.

Harry received a commendation for his work and was promoted to Chief Inspector in charge of domestic abuse cases.

5

HIS DARKENED MINISTRY

The Reverend Alfred Warburton walked into his church at 6.00 am. His walk from the rectory to the church was about 500 yards. At this time of day, with the sun beginning to rise and the birds singing a full dawn chorus, Alfred enjoyed his short walk. It gave him time to consider the upcoming day's events. Two weddings and a funeral. He smiled inwardly at himself. It reminded him of a film of the same name. Or was that four weddings? He couldn't remember.

Alfred was reaching sixty years old. He'd been in the Catholic ministry since he was nineteen. Since then, he looked at the oaths he'd taken as a young priest seriously. He was celibate, something which, when he was younger, became a serious hormonal problem, mainly when young women who regarded him as handsome almost threw themselves at him. He found it difficult to remain chaste.

His current ministry in the little village of Knightsbrook, nestled in the Cotswold hills, included a vast four-bedroom rectory built in the sixteenth century, about the same time as the church. Although he enjoyed the house's architecture, he felt it was far too big for him and would have preferred something smaller. But that would not be the case.

He had become disillusioned with the Church, his faith, and his ministry. He contemplated hanging up his rosary beads and retreating to—well, anywhere but where he was.

His church, saved from destruction during the Reformation, became Protestant and was given back to the Catholic church many years later.

An edifice with a chancel and two lady chapels, the architecture of the church he had never been in dispute with. It was the growing politics and the Church's interference in government that he was in disagreement with.

At this time of the morning, the silence in the church had a calming effect on the jumble of thoughts racing through his mind and making his ability to concentrate nigh on impossible. He had no one he could trust to talk to. His parents, both of the cloth, had passed away years ago, and his best friend had died in a car accident two years ago.

Yes, his parishioners were helpful, kind and caring, but they seemed to be out for what they could get. A trope that seemed more prevalent every day. Not everyone, of course – only those who were the most vociferous of his dwindling congregation.

Unlocking the church, he entered through the vestry door. Since it was not quite light, he didn't turn on any lights. He knew his way by heart. Walking into the body of the church, he bowed reverently at the altar before moving to his pew.

He took up a large, black, soft-backed bible and turned it to the page he'd marked. He began reading:

John 16:33 I have said these things to you, that in me you may have peace. I'm the world you will have tribulation. But take heart ...'

A slight noise at the back of the church drew his attention towards the main church doors. A shuffling, like something being scraped along the floor, like a cassock. No. There wouldn't be anyone here at this time of the morning.

Alfred put down his bible and went to investigate. Stopping close to the confessionals, he heard it again. Now streaming through chancel windows, the sun lit the church in an effusion of colour. Dust particles in the air glistened like tiny fireflies.

Out of the corner of his eye, he thought he saw movement. Something was coming at him fast. He may be out of shape, but he still had it in him to bring his burglar down by tripping him up.

The burglar sprawled on the floor. He was wearing a heavy, floor-length wool coat that looked far too big for him. Underneath the coat, he wore a blue lumberjack-type patterned shirt and dirty jeans. He held his hands up.

'I've stolen nothin'.'

'How do I know that?' Alfred said.

'Look at me, I couldn't carry anythin'.'

'Stand up and empty your pockets.'

The burglar did as he was told. The coat he was wearing dragged on the floor. At about five-foot-five, the coat hid his wiry frame.

'Why are you here?'

'I need sanctuary in a church of God.'

'Are you being chased or hunted by someone?'

'I might be.'

Alfred had heard all this before. People always thought claiming sanctuary in a church automatically allowed them to live in.

'You either are or not, one of the two.'

'The police,' he confided reluctantly.

'Why are they chasing you?'

'I cannot tell you. You're a priest.'

'Do you want to confess to something?'

'I'm not a Catholic.'

'Do you feel that is a bar for you to confess?'

'I suppose not.'

'Well then?'

The man in the long coat confessed everything. At first, Alfred didn't want to believe a word of it. The man, who called himself Robert, not Bob, had told him several stories that, if true, Alfred would be unsure how or whether he should receive absolution from his sins. And *if* true, there were many.

Even he would not be allowed into the Kingdom of Heaven in the knowledge of what he had done to spend the rest of his days in damnation.

Robert had nowhere to stay. Alfred had plenty of room at the rectory, but after what he had told him, could he offer him the sanctuary he'd demanded?

Of course, he couldn't, but that would be inhumane. The man needed rest and food. Must he help this man, or was he putting himself at risk?

For now, he told Robert he could remain in the church. He hoped he might be happy with that and then disappear overnight.

A bit later, Alfred took Robert a bowl of soup and some bread, for which he appeared grateful, and later again took him some blankets. He had to ask him. 'What do you intend to do now?'

'I don't know,' Robert replied. 'Whatever happens, I will end up in the nick.'

'Why not give yourself up? Now. This evening, I can absolve you of your crimes. It could go better for you.'

'There is something else I need to do first.'

Alfred stared at Robert.

'No, Vicar, not as bad as I've just confessed to you.'

'But bad,' Alfred commented. 'You'll be leaving, then?'

'Do you want me to go?'

'You cannot stay here indefinitely.'

Robert laughed. It was not a joyous laugh, Alfred thought.

'I wouldn't wish to,' he said.

'Hmm. I can offer you the sanctuary you require, as you have asked, but I must also ask when you will go.'

'Will you allow me a couple of days?'

Alfred nodded and turned to go. 'You must hand yourself in. You know that?'

Robert bowed his head. 'I will, I promise.'

Two days later, Alfred went to the church to find Robert gone, along with the collection box. There was never too much in there, probably less than a fiver, so he wasn't that worried about it and wouldn't pursue the matter.

In a way, Alfred was relieved that he had left of his own accord. It got him out of the task of having to move him on.

After the evening Mass, Alfred got back to the rectory after dark. No lights were on, but he entered the vast hallway, removed his dog collar, kicked off his shoes, and sighed. Not just because of having to put up with Robert, who reminded him of someone he knew a long time ago, but also because he had to chair the church finance committee and the women's forum.

He padded across the cool ancient flagstones to the kitchen in his socked feet. He still hadn't switched on any lights. It was something that he'd got into the habit of doing. He went to the fridge and opened the door. A shaft of bright light illuminated the kitchen worktop – and the man sitting at the end of the central kitchen island.

'Hello, Reverend.' The voice was low and deep. The light hadn't reached his face, but the long coat gave him away.

'How did you get in, Robert?'

'I have some skills in that regard,' he said. You could hear the smile in his voice.

'I thought you'd gone.'

'I was going but have one more thing to do, so I took you up on your offer.'

'What offer?'

'For me to stay here with you.' The face, now revealed, smiled again. A cold, sinister smile that held no warmth.

'I told you. You cannot stay here.'

'Who's going to know?'

'Me!'

'That's unimportant.'

'Unimportant!' Alfred exclaimed, angered.

'Let's have a review of your life.'

'I don't need a review of my life, thank you.'

'I think you do.'

'How do you come to think that? I've known you less than a week.'

Alfred, who had been holding the fridge door open, let it close, plunging the kitchen into darkness. He switched on the lights.

Robert was gone.

For the rest of the evening, Alfred paced the rectory in an attempt to find Robert. Finally, he sat down at his laptop and searched for "Robert," "Murder," and "Escape." Nothing relevant appeared, and then he remembered that the local police wanted him.

He called the police on 101 and eventually got through to a detective. He asked him what he knew about Robert.

'Have you spoken to him recently?' the detective asked.

'About three hours ago. He broke into my house.'

'But he's not with you now?'

'No, after a brief conversation, he left.'

'To go where?'

Alfred shrugged his shoulders and said, 'Could be anywhere.'

'Are you sure he's still not in your house?'

'I'm sure I've searched everywhere for him.'

The detective sounded frustrated on the phone. 'Very well. If he comes back, you need to let us know immediately.'

'What's he done?' Alfred said as if he didn't know.

'Some terrible things, Reverend. That's all you need to know. Call us, please.' And the detective put the phone down.

ALFRED RETIRED TO BED EARLY. He was confused and unhappy. What Robert had told him in the confessional had frozen him to the core, not just physically but also in his faith.

In all his years as a priest, he had never encountered such criminal behaviour from another human being.

He faced a dichotomy of conflict: one for obtaining justice for the victim's family and one for the sanctity of the confession.

What he should and shouldn't do was only confirmation of the melee of thoughts swimming around in his head. He'd had these conflicts before, but not on this scale. It was a time when he was younger in the ministry, and everything to him then was clear. Now older and wiser, Alfred reflected on his faith and the society in which he lived. Even the children in his Sunday School classes were different now. They were more forthright, more aggressive in their outlook and got their way by making it quite plain what they would do if he or anyone else upset them.

He wondered how much longer humanity would survive. There had never been so many conflicts in the years since the end of World War Two. Everyone seemed to fight everyone and ninety per cent of the time; they were about different religious faiths.

He put his head in his hands and wept. Eventually falling asleep – restless, haunted.

THE MORNING CAME in dull and overcast, and a sense of foreboding filled the air and his mind. To wash away this feeling, he had a cold shower, dried himself off vigorously, and returned to his bedroom across the landing. As he did so, a pleasant and pungent smell of bacon drifted up the stairs.

Alfred froze. His housekeeper wasn't due in today. Then, with a frightening thought, he knew that the only other person it could be was Robert raiding his fridge for food. He wondered whether he should call that detective. He went into his bedroom and hastily got dressed.

Making his way downstairs, his cold shower had invigorated his body and he was up for anything. This time, he would physically throw him out if he had to.

Alfred entered the kitchen. He saw Robert sitting at the end of the central bar with a plate of fried eggs, bacon, coffee, and other condiments.

'I thought you'd gone, Robert?'

'Well, I came back.'

'You can't stay.'

'But I demanded sanctuary.'

'I'm not prepared to give it to you. So I want you to leave. Now!'

'Well. I'm not prepared to,' he sneered.

'You need to hand yourself into the police, or I will call them myself.'

'And what are you going to tell them, eh? You can't tell them what I said, can you? So what'll you do?' he scoffed.

Alfred thought for a moment. 'I've already told them, actually.'

Robert put down his knife and fork, standing up from the bar and walking towards Alfred.

'What have you told them?' he said with deepening hostility.

'That you're here and that you have sanctuary.'

'And what do they want you to do?'

'Just tell them when you leave. Which is now, by the way.'

'You need to think about your past before you follow this path, Alfred.'

'What has my past got to do with you being a murderer?'

'You'll have to think very hard.'

Robert returned to his plate, finished the only piece of bacon, and drained his coffee. Retrieving his coat from the back of the bar stool, he said, 'I'm going to leave now and let you think about your past sins. I'll be back for dinner later.'

Robert left the kitchen, and Alfred listened as he walked across the hallway. The front door opened and slammed closed.

Apart from being extremely riled by Robert, he was also perplexed. He understood nothing about what Robert was saying about his past sins. What was that all about? He'd been a servant of God all his life. What on earth could he mean?

LATER THAT SAME AFTERNOON, he received a visit from the local parish constable. Having offered him tea and biscuits, he said, 'How can I help you, officer?'

'It is me who can help you, padre.'

'How come?'

'We have received information that you recently had a visitor to your church.'

'And how did you come by that information?'

'One of your parishioners reported seeing a tramp-like man enter the church. We want to know if you have any knowledge of this?'

'I do, yes. He was sleeping rough. I allowed him to stay in the church for a couple of nights. He demanded the ancient right of sanctuary.'

'And where is he now?'

Alfred shrugged his shoulders. 'I went to the church this morning, and he wasn't there.' It was partially the truth, he thought.

'You think he's gone?'

Alfred gave a brief nod.

'You don't seem so sure.'

'Well, unless he comes back this evening. I'm not his keeper.'

'I understand.'

The constable got up to leave when he heard the front door open. A man called Alfred's name. He recognised the voice. What was he going to do now? Before he could stop the officer, he was out in the hallway and came face to face with Robert.

'Is this the man we were just speaking about?'

'It is, yes.'

'He's moved into the rectory, then?'

'No, that is not the case.'

Robert turned to go.

'Wait a minute,' the officer said. 'Don't I know you?'

Robert responded by heading for the door.

'Don't walk away from me, sir. I need a word.'

Robert bolted for the door, flung it open, and ran for his life. The officer, burdened by all the kit he had to carry around his torso, gave chase. But, of course, nobody can run faster than those running from the law.

The officer soon gave up and resorted to pulling out his radio and barking an out-of-breath message to his colleagues to be on the lookout for Robert.

He returned to Alfred, who stood waiting by the front door.

'I think we need another chat?' the officer said, a little pissed off.

They walked back into the rectory.

'Tell me, padre, who is this man to you?'

'He's a vagrant who entered my church asking for sanctuary.'

'Is that still a thing?' the officer said.

'If you mean whether a person can still seek sanctuary in a church of God – yes, it's still a thing,' Alfred said with a contemptuous smile.

'What did he tell you?'

'Nothing I can tell you, officer.'

'And why not?'

'He confessed to me. It's confidential. A secret, even.'

'If he admitted a capital crime, which I believe he has, do you not have a duty to keep your community safe?'

'Unfortunately, under the seal of the confessional, I cannot tell you.'

'Surely, in this day and age, you can no longer do that?'

'Sanctuary and the confession pre-dates Christianity, officer, and under Canon 983.1, the sacramental seal is inviolable and forbids me to betray the penitent in words or any other manner for any reason.'

'Have you just absolved him of his crimes with a couple of Hail Marys?' the constable said with disdain.

'I see you are unaware of the Catholic faith and its traditions.'

'I'm not aware of any faith, to be honest, padre. To me, it's all a load of hogwash.'

'Although you are an atheist, it makes no difference to me. I still cannot tell you.'

'Let me put it like this. A failure to divulge what the man told you about his crimes will make you an accessory after the fact. So it's in your interest to tell me.'

'I cannot.'

'Did you absolve him?'

'For someone who doesn't believe in all this "hogwash", you certainly have the right terms of phrase. And no. I didn't.'

'Why?'

'He refused to repent for his sins and showed he wouldn't change his ways. Do you know who he is and what he's done?'

'We know both, yes.'

'You know, then, that it would be difficult for him to repent.'

'Whether or not he does, he'll still be in gaol for the rest of his life.' The officer looked fed up with the conversation and turned to go. 'When you have decided to co-operate with us, please get in touch with us. I will report this conversation to my supervisors about your lack of help.'

'You do what you have to. It does not and will not change anything.'

The officer opened the front door, took one last look at Alfred and stepped out into the sunshine. He left the door open. Alfred watched him walk towards his police car, climb in and leave the rectory grounds. He closed the door.

Alfred knew what Robert had done, or at least been accused of doing, needed punishment and castigating. Walking into his study, he collected his bible and turned to Judges 17:6:

"In those days there was no King in Israel, but everyman did that which was right in his own eyes."

He mulled the passage over in his mind. *"That which was right."* What is right? he thought. What was right for him might not be right for someone else, especially a police officer who desperately wanted to get Robert's confession. This was something he really did not want to think about. The description given by Robert was enough to turn Alfred's stomach just thinking about it.

The light faded as he sat in his study, reading more scriptures. He put the desk lamp on and decided to get some more church paperwork done. It wasn't paperwork, really, because it was all done on his laptop now.

A bottle of wine stood on his desk, the top screwed on. He picked it up, unscrewed the top and poured the dregs into the used wine glass next to it.

He leaned back in the plush leather-winged office chair and sipped the wine. It had gone tart—well, it had been open for a few days.

The noise from the window made him jump as a large piece of metal came crashing through the window and impaled itself in the Chesterfield settee.

He jumped up and went to the window. Alfred realised he was shaking. Looking out, he saw nothing. He knew who it was and knew that it was a bad sign for him if Robert had taken this stance against him now.

Robert told him to think about his sins and that he knew him. Robert didn't remind him of anyone in his past or present. What did he mean?

After he'd finished looking out the window, peering into the darkness to see some movement, he drew the curtains and turned in for the night. He didn't feel like eating anything now.

THE HAMMERING AWOKE Alfred from a deep sleep and worked its way into his consciousness. At first, he thought it was a dream, but as he awoke, he realised that someone was banging on the front door.

Hauling himself out of bed, he threw on his dressing gown and went downstairs.

'Yes, yes. I'm coming,' he called as he walked down the stairs.

Alfred looked at the grandmother's clock in the hallway, glancing at the time – 6.20 am. Really!

He unlocked and opened the front door, not knowing what to expect. Seeing half a dozen police officers outside the front door was a shock.

A detective was standing at the front of the hoard. He held up his warrant card.

'I'm Detective Chief Inspector Randall, Reverend, and we have a warrant to search the premises.'

'Why? What are you looking for?'

'We have reason to believe you are harbouring a dangerous criminal.'

Alfred looked dumbfounded. 'I told the constable – him, standing behind you – that Robert had gone after he chased after him. He hasn't been back to my knowledge.'

'We still have to make the search.' Randall took a step forward.

Alfred stood aside to let the officers in.

'Don't break anything, or you'll have the church on your neck,' he said as they entered and dispersed themselves around the rectory.

'Can we talk, please?' Randall said.

Alfred waved him into the kitchen. 'I need a coffee,' he said. 'You?'

Randall nodded. 'Very kind. Thank you.'

'You won't find him here, Chief Inspector. He's not been back since that cop chased him.'

'I understand, but we have to do this.'

Alfred nodded as he put Randall's mug of coffee on the table in front of him. They sat down.

'What do you know of this man, Reverend?'

'Nothing. He turned up at the church. I gave him sanctuary, that's all.'

'But I understand you had a confession from him?'

'You know I can't tell you that, Inspector.'

'Did he confess to crimes he committed?'

'And as I keep saying. I can't tell you anything about what he said in the confessional. You know that. So why ask?'

'But, as I understand it, there are circumstances, say in the case of murder, when you may divulge information.'

'No. Never.'

'Never!'

'No.'

'That's not how I understand it.'

'And just what do you understand?'

'That confessed capital crimes, under the circumstances, can be told to the authorities.'

'That is not right. It'd be bad for me.'

'In what way?'

'*Latae sententiae*.'

'What?'

'Ex-communication. That would happen to me if I told you what he said in that box.'

'There must be something you can give me, Reverend?'

'It is a crime under God to break the seal of the confession. I can't say anymore, Inspector. If I could, I would believe me. What he told me has given me sleepless nights.'

'Then unburden yourself to me.' Randall smiled.

'You sound like my counsellor, Inspector. I'm bound. There is nothing I can do.'

'Would you like to see this man do it again?'

'Of course not.'

'Then tell me what he said.'

Alfred turned away, got up from the table and stared out the kitchen window. The sun was rising across the church tower. Still looking out of the window, he said, 'I can tell you, outside of the confessional, that he told me to think about my sins and that he knew who I was.'

'And do you know him?'

'No. Not that I recall.'

'How far back is he going in these allegations of whatever they are?'

Alfred shrugged.

'How long have you been a priest?'

'I entered the service of God when I was sixteen.'

'Parents?'

'Both dead.'

'Orphan?'

Alfred nodded.

'Brothers. Sisters.'

Alfred shook his head.

'Girlfriend. Boyfriend?'

'I have had several lady friends, but no one at the moment, or likely to have at my age.'

'Many people of your age can still find love, Reverend.' Randall smiled.

A side Alfred didn't expect to see from the policeman in front of him. He turned back to Randall. After further thought, he said, 'I think I may know why he came here.'

'And?'

'I've been thinking constantly about what he said to me. That I should consider my sins. Even as priests, none of us are perfect. We have always held ourselves morally on the high ground. Looked upon as pillars of society.'

'Not so much now,' Randall said. 'A lot has happened in all the churches of God.'

'I know, and that in itself gives pause for thought. Even if it is deliberately overlooked even by the Holy See.'

'Carry on.'

'Well, when I was in seminary, training as a priest, there was one individual whom everyone wondered why he wanted to join the priesthood. He was disruptive, anti-establishment and advocated against many of the Catholic traditions, like the use of protection for sex, for example.'

Alfred sat down at the table again. 'I haven't thought about this in years. But it's the only thing I think he's referring to.'

'What's his name?'

'Robert Dixon.'

'And this is the man who gave you his confession?'

'Well, he introduced himself as Robert, yes.'

'Continue, please.'

'Obviously, his attitude and ideas caught the attention of the powers that be in the seminary. They kept tabs on him. Eventually, he got expelled from the school and ex-communicated. I heard that a few years later, he died in a boating accident.'

'What did he do to get expelled?'

'The headmaster at the school used to keep exotic birds— noisy little buggers when you're trying to pray. So Dixon let them all out. Those that came back, he killed them.'

'A psychopath in the making, then,' Randall commented.

'Indeed,' Alfred agreed.

'Where do you come in all this, then?'

'I was the one who got him expelled and probably ex-communicated. You see, I was with him when he let the birds out, so to him, my sin was to blab it all out to the cardinal so I didn't get the same punishment.'

'Surely that wasn't enough for him to search you out?'

'I don't think he knew I was here.'

'You think he stumbled across you, then realised who you were when he saw you?'

'Seems that way, yes.'

'Any idea where he might hide out?'

'Woods behind the church would be my guess.'

As the conversation ended, a uniformed police sergeant confirmed that the house search was complete and nothing unusual had been found. Randall thanked him and sent the team off to search the woods.

Randall finished his coffee and got up from the table.

'Thank you, Reverend, for the coffee and your co-operation. But I still need access to that confession.' He smiled. They shook hands.

'Never going to happen,' Alfred said.

Two DAYS PASSED before Alfred heard any more about Robert Dixon. He tried to put the last week out of his mind. He couldn't help but think that it wasn't over. The DCI had rung him on both days, asking whether he had heard or seen anything further about his whereabouts. It was clear to Alfred that the detective had no reason to believe him, but that's detectives for you.

DCI Randall turned up at the rectory just after six on the third day. Alfred invited him in, and Randall's face looked grim as he stood at the front door.

He took a seat in Alfred's study. The hole in the Chesterfield was evident. Alfred offered Randall a drink, which he accepted.

'To what do I owe this pleasure, Detective?'

'I thought I would let you know how our investigation into Robert Dixon is progressing.'

'And ... how is it going?'

'I have to say that it isn't going well.'

'He's still free,' Alfred remarked.

Randall nodded.

'And you don't know where?'

Randall shook his head, then said, 'Well, yes and no.'

'What does that mean?'

'We tracked him to a private airfield near Banbury. Then his phone got switched off. It was intermittent at the best of times. It was good luck that we picked him up when we did.'

'Probably a deliberate act,' Alfred said.

'Possibly. But since that time, the phone has been off.'

'I didn't think he had a phone. Are you sure it was him?'

'We're ninety per cent certain. One of his "associates" gave us the heads up in a deal to get him out of lock-up.' Randall smiled. 'The current theory is that he's absconded from the UK, so we've issued an international arrest warrant.'

'Whatever happens, then, I'm going to be looking over my shoulder till you find him.'

Randall nodded. 'We will continue to search for where he is, but it could take some time. Years, probably, if he disappears in any country outside of the EU.'

Alfred got up from his chair and poured both of them another drink.

'That's all we can do now, Reverend,' Randall said.

'Alfred, please, Detective.'

'Fletcher, Alfred.'

'My stake in the Church is diminished because of this and other incidents over the years.'

'What do you mean by that?'

'I have become disillusioned by the dark ministry it has become.'

'Ah, so you can tell me what Dixon said,' Randall snickered.

Alfred smiled at Randall, pointing at him. 'You keep trying your luck, Fletcher!'

'Can't help a man for trying.'

'All I will say is that he *really* needs to be caught. He is an evil man - capable of anything.'

The evening with Randall continued in a convivial atmosphere. They agreed to meet again and occasionally "chew the cud," Randall called it.

Alfred retired to bed at about 1:00 a.m. after Randall had left. He felt he had made a friend with whom he could talk, relate, and trust. He went to sleep happy, knowing that his life may be looking up.

He woke at 3.30 am. He saw, standing over him, a man in a long brown woollen coat.

6

A HAUNTING AT CLOVERLEAF HOUSE

1942

Alice was frantically searching the upstairs rooms for her sister. The fire had started when the German bombers dropped their payload on what Alice called the East Wing of the house before they reached the English Channel.

'Mattie! Mattie! Where are you? Mattie, come on, we have to get out of here. Now!'

The Edwardian manor house stood atop a hill overlooking the Strait of Dover. Alice and Mattie had watched the approaching German bombers earlier in the evening, never knowing that they would cause utter destruction as they returned to France.

Cloverleaf House had been the family home for many years, long before Mattie and Alice were born. They lived with their mother and father and a staff of three or four, depending on the time of year. Both parents were away working for the war effort in London, and the bombings there did not help Mattie and

Alice, knowing that they were under the barrage of explosions and fires.

'Mattie!' Alice continued to call out to her sister. Alice dropped to the floor as the smoke reached into her lungs, depriving her of the vital oxygen needed to sustain life. She covered her face with her torn white poplin nightdress. She crawled along the landing towards the last room where she hoped her sister might be.

At twelve years old, she had become a surrogate mother to her younger five-year-old sister and knew that it was her job to get her out. But where was she? She had not been in her room, where she had left her earlier in the evening when they had said good night.

The bombs had dropped at around 1.00 am, shaking the house to its foundations and rocking the west wing where they had their bedrooms. She assumed that both the housekeeper and driver, who looked after them while their parents were away, had perished when the bombs landed.

It was up to her now. She had to find her sister. Where on earth was she? 'Mattie!' she called out as loud as her smoked-filled throat would allow. The stench of burning furniture and wood was also getting down her throat. Still no reply. The deafening roar of the fire that had now fully engulfed the house was licking around the landing where she was.

Alice was now frightened for her life and unable to find her sister. Her heart pounding in her chest, she crawled to the last room where she thought her sister would be, not thinking about how they were going to get out. She pushed her way through the door, which stood ajar

Debris fell everywhere as the house slowly disintegrated around her. She thought she could hear the bells of the approaching fire engine coming up the hill to their rescue.

As she entered the room, she could just about see the

silhouette of her sister slumped in the room's corner. Her eyes were closed, and she was not moving. The pains in her chest were increasing as she was finding it harder and harder to breathe. Still on her hands and knees, she crawled to her sister to check if she was still alive, but there was no response. The noise was deafening; the fire was closing in on both of them, and it was there that she realised that neither of them was going to escape.

Suddenly, and without warning, the floor beneath them gave way. Gathering up her sister in her arms, she waited for the inevitable disintegration of the floor. She knew nothing about that as she slipped into unconsciousness before the ultimate oblivion enveloped them both.

Spring 2025

Pushing through the undergrowth at the top of the Dover Downs, Sally came across the shell of a house. She moved some debris away from the front entrance and found an old sign, upon which was displayed in faded writing, "Cloverleaf House".

'Ben, come look at this,' Sally shouted at her new husband of three weeks. In the intervening seventy-plus years since its bombing, the house had been left for its owners to return to restore it, but they never did. Now almost reclaimed by nature, the shell of the house stood in the gloom of the approaching stormy weather out in the Channel.

In the mid-1980s, the local council wanted to tear it down, but searching for any relatives of the owners was fruitless, and they could never agree on what they wanted to do with it. It got left and virtually forgotten.

Although the house was not the biggest country house in the world, extensive restoration would undoubtedly make it a pleasant family home. Although the restoration would cost a pretty penny, Ben thought it might be worth it. The front face of the house looked out over the Channel Port of Dover, now a bustling hub and gateway to France. On a day like today, Ben had to admit that the view over the Channel was superb.

Ben followed Sally through the bracken and the almost impenetrable Japanese Knotweed. The undergrowth had made a complete mess of Sally's hair.

'Jesus, Sally. I've just ripped my shirt climbing through that lot.'

She ignored the comment. 'Look at this, though.'

Both stood in front of what should have been the front door, looking up at the shells of the ground and upper floors.

'Well,' said Sally, 'what do you think?'

'I would have preferred something with a roof and windows,' he exclaimed. 'Anyway, it might not be for sale or is owned by the National Trust or something.'

'I know, we could find out, couldn't we,' Sally said, pleading. 'Look at the views. Imagine sitting in the garden and looking out over that.' She waved her arms as she took in the whole vista that was the Strait of Dover.

'It'll take an awful lot of restoration, even if it could be rebuilt and if we could get our hands on it.'

'But what if we could? That restoration project we were talking about? And it'd be great for the children.' She scrambled towards the front entrance, leaving Ben pondering on her last comment. He followed her into what should have been the entrance hallway. An ash tree had grown from the hallway and towered above both of them, up through where the first-floor ceiling and the roof had once been. Ben stood with his new wife, looking up towards the west side of the house. He felt a strange and tingly feeling run down his spine and couldn't decide whether that was a good feeling or one of foreboding.

He erred on the side of good. 'You know,' he said, putting an arm around his wife's waist, 'I think you're right. Let's see if we can find out about it.'

As they went to leave the entrance and fight their way back through the undergrowth, Ben glanced down to the bottom of the garden, reflecting on what it may have looked like in its heyday.

At the bottom of the garden was a large oak tree, from which hung a child's swing. He walked on, but out of the corner of his eye, he could have sworn that the swing was moving - swinging - as if being used. He thought no more about it, and they returned to their hotel.

AFTER A LONG AND drawn-out legal process, Cloverleaf House was finally in the hands of Ben and Sally. Work on restoration soon started, and despite some setbacks - an unexploded German bomb being one of them - they finally moved in two years later. Only weeks after moving in, Sally found out she was pregnant.

Ben had spent some time researching the house's history in the local archives and was keen to tell Sally all about it when he got home.

Sitting in their new lounge, Ben said, 'I did some research on the house today.'

'Anything interesting?' Sally said as she brought in a tray of pasta for them both.

'Yes. Seems the place has a bit of a history. It belonged to a family called the Martiniques. It was a family home for a couple of generations. They farmed the land around it until it got sold to the next-door farm after old man Martinique couldn't farm the land anymore. He'd lost a lot of his labourers in the first world war. There were enough employees to form one of those private companies. Unfortunately, none of them came back.'

'That's terrible,' Sally exclaimed.

'It gets worse. Old man Martinque's son Johnathan took over the house and kept their daughters Alice and Mattie at the house because they thought they'd be safer in Kent than in London.'

'Assuming that during the Blitz, they'd be safe. I can understand that.'

'Then I found this.' Ben showed her a dog-eared press cutting from the Daily Sketch.

COUPLE DEVASTATED AT THE NEWS OF THE DEATH OF THEIR CHILDREN IN KENT.

Lieutenant Commander Johnathan Martinique RN and his wife Abigail were today being comforted by relatives having been notified of the deaths of their children at their family home in Kent, following a German air raid on the town of Dover. Also dying in the house blaze was the house keeper Molly ...

'Four died here overnight, which is why the house was so derelict when we bought it. It got bombed with incendiaries.'

'Hence all the fire damage.'

Ben nodded.

'What happened to Mum and Dad then?'

'Abigail Martinique finished her days in a mental institution after Johnathan went down with his ship in the North Atlantic about six months before the end of the war.'

'That's such a tragic story,' Sally said. 'So that's why nothing happened to the house. Nobody to pass it on to.'

'I hope we can turn this into a cheerful house, Sal,' Ben said.

He closed the files from which he'd been reading and took them into his study. Returning to the kitchen, he poured himself a glass of water, then said, 'I'm going to bed. You coming?'

They both went to bed early, but Ben woke with a start at about 1.00 am. Despite the warmth of the early spring, the room had a decided chill. Sally had curled herself up in the duvet, which probably accounted for Ben being cold. But no, this was something different. Something that Ben had not felt since he was a child. Thinking no more about it, he tried to cuddle closer to Sally, but the duvet was so tightly "packed" around her that he decided he'd better find a blanket. He manoeuvred himself towards the edge of his side of the bed, trying not to wake his pregnant wife.

Turning over to get out of bed, he was startled to be confronted by the shimmering outline of a young girl gazing at him. Her eyes were dark and sunken into the sockets. Mixed with the blood-smeared face were tears and soot marks. The girl seemed to say something, but he could not make it out. Ben could smell the stench of burning flesh, which turned his stomach, but the picture before him faded away. He did not know what to make of it. Was this real, or was he dreaming? He turned back to his wife and saw that she was still asleep. When he turned back, whatever it was he saw had gone. The chill had gone from the room, and it was tranquil.

Ben got out of bed and walked to the bedroom window, where he sat down on the window ledge and looked out over the garden. As he stared out, he saw the girl sitting on the swing at the bottom of the garden. Was it the same girl, he wondered? He moved away from the window ledge and sat down on the chair in front of it. Wrapping himself in his dressing gown and a blanket, he eventually fell asleep.

At breakfast the following morning, Ben was in a reflective mood.

'Everything all right, love?' Sally said as she breezed into the kitchen. She had been up early and prepared a breakfast of fresh coffee and poached eggs on toast for them both. She put the plate on the table in front of him. He just stared at it.

'Well, I know I'm not a gourmet chef,' she said, 'but it's not that bad, surely?'

'Pardon?' Ben replied.

'The poached eggs,' Sally exclaimed, pointing to them on the table in front of him.

'Oh, sorry, love, miles away. No, these are great, thanks.'

They both ate their breakfast, making nothing but small talk. Sally could see that Ben was preoccupied and left it be. She knew he'd come around to telling her in his own time.

Sally got up from the table.

'How did you sleep?' Ben asked as she walked to the kitchen sink and rinsed the plates before putting them in the dishwasher.

'Okay. I was bushed. We shouldn't have had all that alcohol as you recounted the history of this place – not in my condition.' She looked down and rubbed her belly. Turning side-on to Ben, she said, 'Can you see it yet?'

Ben chuckled, lightening the mood a little. 'No, not yet, but I'll tell you when I can.'

Sally finished rinsing the breakfast dishes and sat down at the table again. 'Yes,' she continued. 'I slept well. How about you?'

'Well, until you nicked all the duvet, I was fine.'

'Yes, sorry about that. Got chilly.'

'So, you noticed, then.'

'Noticed what?'

'How cold it got in the bedroom.'

'Well, yes, I suppose it's bound to get chilly early in the morning.'

Ben looked down at the table, wondering whether he

should tell his wife what he saw last night. He knew she was the sort of person who would not believe it until she saw it herself or someone could supply verifiable evidence. As a lawyer, that's all she had to work with, and sometimes it spilled over into her personal life regarding uncertainties. Still, she'd have to know, eventually.

'I saw her,' he started.

'Saw who?'

'A little girl.'

'What little girl?'

'I haven't told you this, but do you remember that day when we first found this place?'

'Yes,' Sally said with some concern in her voice. 'How could I forget? You complained about ripping your shirt all the way back to the hotel.' She smiled. It wasn't an admonishment.

Ben looked down at his empty plate, then said quietly, 'Just as we were leaving, I thought I saw a tree swing at the bottom of the garden moving back and forth as if someone was on it. I had that feeling it was a little girl.'

'Why didn't you tell me this at the time?'

'Because I dismissed it as my imagination.'

'Were you imagining it again last night, or was it just the drink you'd had playing tricks on your mind?'

'No, it wasn't my imagination; I saw her face. It was as close to me as you are and just as tangible.'

Sally sat and stared into Ben's eyes. 'You are kidding me. I mean, nobody believes in all that paranormal stuff, surely. We're in the twenty-first century. It's all debunked anyway.'

Ben averted his eyes from Sally. He knew that this would be difficult.

'I saw her face; it was blooded, covered in soot, and she had been crying. How can I make this stuff up? I'm not exactly that imaginative, for God's sake!'

Sally stood up, turning her back on Ben, trying not to giggle. 'So you're telling me that this place is haunted.' She gave a ghostly *wooooo,* and the stifled giggle came out.

'Well, I am telling you what happened, and you can believe me or not.'

'I'm not saying I don't believe you, love, but you know I don't believe in all that shit.'

'What if I can prove it to you?'

'Well, good luck to you because nobody has done it yet, not even Danny Robins on *Uncanny.* I'm on team sceptic, by the way.'

'So cynical. It would be best if you opened your mind to possibilities other than evidential facts,' he said sharply.

Sally shot him a disapproving glance.

'Sorry, that was uncalled for. It's just troubling me, that's all.'

After the conversation in the kitchen, Ben felt slightly disappointed that Sally had not been more supportive of his story. She had left to go to work, leaving Ben alone in the house.

The house felt suddenly quiet again. He listened to the light breeze blowing outside, but all was silent in the house. This he couldn't understand. There was always some creaking and groaning from most houses he had lived in, but this silence was almost deafening. He needed to take his mind off the earlier conversation with his wife. He wasn't due to return to work for another week.

Finishing his coffee, he went upstairs to change. He decided he'd start on the garden, as it was a nice, dry, sunny day, and cleared some overgrowth.

Out in the garden, he instinctively made his way to the large oak tree at the bottom of the once expansive area laid to lawn. He wandered through the undergrowth with spade and scythe in hand. The spade he had brought from his old house, but the scythe Ben found on the grounds while it was being renovated, was in remarkably good condition. He looked up at the old oak tree and estimated it would have to be over a hundred years old, at the very least. 'I wonder what things you have seen in this garden over the years,' he muttered.

As he stood looking at the tree with his back to the house, the knurled and ancient tree seemed to bow in deference to him in the light breeze. The breeze rustling the leaves was captivating and somehow calming, putting his conversation with Sally out of his mind.

To his left, he saw a low bough upon which hung the remnant of a garden swing. The seat he found buried in the undergrowth, rotting and full of bugs and insects. Some of the heavy hemp rope had also rotted away. The tree had engulfed the rope knots that had held the swing in place as it grew and waited for someone to bring the garden back to life.

Nobody could have sat on this swing, he thought. On seeing the girl on the swing last night, his nightmare returned. He cleared an area around the bottom of the tree with the scythe and sat down. As he did so, he became acutely aware that he was being watched, or at least it felt like it. He could neither see nor hear anyone nearby, and the house and garden were miles away from neighbours.

He sat and looked out at the house. It had taken two years to renovate it completely. The destruction caused by the wartime bombs and the ensuing fire had damaged the foundations more than their fair share. The fact that it had virtually been left since then ensured that any renovation would not be straightforward.

He was grateful that he had moved his money out of the stock market before the crash of 2008. He also appreciated that Sally had contributed to the renovation, which made it *home*. The renovation cost far more than they'd budgeted, topping out at just over 1.2 million, reducing his investment portfolio to a mere fraction of its original size.

Shaking himself out of his reverie, he got up from leaning back on the tree and leapt into action. Cutting backwards and forwards with the scythe, digging out deep-rooted weeds. By midmorning, he was halfway up the garden and had made a massive pile of undergrowth ready for burning.

He found some delineation between grass and border and was working his way up the right-hand side of the garden, digging and turning the border area, when his spade struck something metallic. He stooped to see what it was and moved some earth away to discover he'd hit a small metal box tied with string, which disintegrated when he touched it. He saw it was an old brown MacFarlane Lang biscuit tin with the faded picture of a young girl in a white gown and blue sash on the lid. He wiped the earth off with his hands and looked it over, wondering whether it could have been a time capsule put there by the previous owners. It might even give him some ideas about them or try to identify the ghostly images he kept seeing.

He walked back to the house with the box under his arm. The watched feeling returned and as he walked into the house, for a moment, he thought he could hear the sound of children playing and laughing. But again, he dismissed this as his imagination.

After setting the box down on the large pine kitchen table, he switched on the kettle and made himself a cup of coffee. He then sat at the table, studying the box for a long time.

'Aren't you going to open it, then?'

Startled, he looked up to see a large man standing in the kitchen doorway.

'Who are you, and how did you get into my house?' he questioned the man standing in the doorway.

'The back door was open. I knocked, but you couldn't have heard me. May I come in?'

Ben nodded to the man. He strode into the kitchen, and Ben extended his right hand. The man didn't take it.

'Hello,' he said. 'I'm Fred. We farm the fields around here.'

'Been doing it long, then?'

'Yes, took over from my old dad; been farming these fields for about a hundred and fifty years.'

'Oh ... right, your dad must have known the previous owners of this house then?'

'Yes, he knew the Martinique family well.'

'Do you know much about the house and who lived here? Only I am trying to find out myself. Bit of historical research about the place as we've restored it.' Ben didn't want to let on that he was researching a ghost story, just in case he got the same reaction from Fred as from Sally earlier in the day.

'I don't know too much, but I know that the two children who lived here with the housekeeper and the driver all died in the house. Bombed during the Second World War.'

'All of them ... *died* in this house?'

'Yes, that's right, did you not know?'

'We recently found out after I'd done some research. We know the house got bombed during the war, but didn't know anyone had died in here until we'd moved in.' Ben indicated for Fred to sit down at the table. He remained standing.

'They should have told you that,' he said.

They both studied the tin for a short time.

'What do you think is in the tin, then?' Ben asked Fred, who was now studying it intently. Ben pulled it closer to him.

'Probably something the children put in the garden when they were here,' he suggested.

'Don't know whether I should open it,' he questioned himself.

'Well, I'll leave you to ponder on that. I need to get back to work.'

'Okay. Thanks for calling in. Any time you're passing, next time, I'll offer you a cup of tea.'

'No, that's okay. Thanks for the offer, though. I'd like to hear how you get on with your research on the house.'

'Yes, yes, okay. Do you have a mobile number I can contact you on?'

'No, don't use them,' Fred said as he strode out the door. 'I'll see you soon.'

In an instance, he was gone, and the house fell silent again.

He wanted to open the box but decided to wait for Sally to get home from work before doing so. After dinner, they sat at the kitchen table with it in front of them.

'Are you going to open it, then, or just stare at it?' Sally remarked.

'I'm not sure I should.'

'And why is that?'

Ben shrugged. 'Just a feeling.'

'About your ghost.' Sally held upon her hands and gave a quotation sign as she said it.

Ben nodded.

'Look, love, it's just a tin, and it's probably full of rubbish and of no significance. Do you want me to open it?'

Ben pushed it towards her. 'Fill yer boots, Mrs Sceptic.'

Sally pulled the box closer to her. She tried to ease the lid off, but it wouldn't budge.

'Might have to get some lubricant on it,' she said.

'Give it here. It can't be that tight on.'

She pushed the box back to him. He grabbed hold of the

box, grasped the lid, and it came off with ease. The lid revealed an old muslin cloth, which he lifted onto the table.

The tin included a set of photographs of the family standing outside the house's front door. The father was wearing a Royal Navy uniform with the rank of Commander, and the mother seemed to be wearing a military uniform, probably ATC. The children stood in front of them, and the father's hand was on the shoulder of the oldest child. All had enormous smiles.

Suddenly, Ben stood up and dropped the photo. He then strode to his study across the hallway and returned with a large magnifying glass. Picking up the photo again, he studied it under the glass before slowly sitting down again.

'Are you alright?' Sally asked. 'It looks like you've seen a ghost.'

'I have,' Ben replied solemnly.

Sally laughed. 'Here we go again. Where is it this time?'

Ben pointed to the photo. 'Here! This girl in the picture is the one I've seen.'

'Ha. More like an overactive imagination, if you ask me.'

'Christ's sake, Sally. If you don't want to believe me, humour me instead of making a big joke. You know that I'm sensitive to this sort of thing.'

He pushed his chair back, scraping it along the kitchen floor. Then, he put the stuff on the table back in the box, closed it, and stormed out of the kitchen.

Sally always knew that Ben was what his mother called a "sensitive"—having a special gift for the esoteric. But Sally found it challenging to comprehend. She'd never seen or felt anything to change her mind on that score.

Sally looked closer at the box, moving it around the table. The patterned top on the box of the young girl seemed to mesmerise her. Could biscuits have come in boxes like this, unlike the paper wrappers they now come in? Deep in thought, she saw a man standing in the doorway.

'Oh ... you gave me a fright,' she said, a bit flustered. 'Who're you, and how did you get in?'

'The door was open. I knocked, but perhaps you didn't hear me.'

'Clearly not,' Sally said, somewhat suspiciously. 'Do we know you?'

'I spoke to your husband yesterday after he had found the box. I thought I'd drop by to see whether you'd opened it?'

'Oh, I see. He said nothing about a visitor.'

'I'm Fred, by the way.'

'Sally.'

'What did you find in the box? Is there anything interesting?'

'Not really, a couple of old photographs. Four people died in this very house, and the parents were away in London.'

'And the pictures?'

'Here, see for yourself.' Sally opened the tin and laid the pictures on the table. Fred leant over to look at them.

'They're fascinating. Everyone who used to live here.'

'If they all died in the bombing, how did this get to be buried in the garden?'

'Well, that's a mystery you will need to discover. Should you want to, of course.'

'Never been that interested in history, but I think Ben will.'

'Ah, that's good then. I think people like to know what happens in these historical cases. So, I'll wish you the best of luck and be on my way. Thanks for letting me look at the contents.'

Fred turned and walked out of the kitchen. Seconds later, Ben came back into the kitchen.

'I'm sorry I got emotional then.'

'That's okay. Did you see Fred on the way in?'

'No. He was here?'

'Yes. He said you met him yesterday.'

Ben nodded.

'Wanted to know what was in the box.'

'Did you show him?'

It was Sally's turn to nod. Ben sat down at the table and opened the box. He took out the picture of the family and their staff. Gathering up the magnifying glass, he looked closely again at the picture. He nodded. 'I thought as much.'

'What? Show me.'

'Look at the guy on the left.'

Sally took the picture and the glass. 'And?'

'Look again.'

'Shut the front door!' Sally exclaimed.

'You, my dear, have just encountered your first ghost. The guy you were talking to was the driver and odd-job man around here. His name was Frederic Winters.'

Sally went as white as a sheet. 'No. It can't be. He was as real as you or me.'

'But he touched nothing. He didn't sit down.'

Sally shook her head.

'Do you believe me now?'

Sally shook her head again. 'There has to be some logical explanation. He's a relative, or he looks like him in the picture—'

'Whose name also happens to be Fred.'

Sally got up from the table. 'I need a drink.' She opened a bottle of wine, filled her glass, and poured another for Ben. Leaning with her back against the sink, she said, 'What the hell do we do now?'

'Nothing. We let it run its course.'

'And if it doesn't?'

Ben shrugged and took a slug of wine. 'Exciting though, isn't it.'

Sally looked nonplussed. 'No, it bloody well isn't. What if it affects our child?'

'I doubt that, to be honest. But let's cross that bridge if we come to it.'

~

THE OPENING of the box saw no further significant encounters with the girl or Fred. Some years later, when Sally had a second child, they began construction work on a new conservatory on the side of the house, and things changed.

They had both been sitting in the garden during the now regular, long, hot summers on the south coast.

Sophie, now four years old, was playing near the old oak tree. Ben had put up a new swing from the thick branch of the oak, and she sat slowly rocking back and forth on it.

When Ben looked at his daughter, it was not just her he saw; she appeared to be talking with another little girl on the swing. He tapped Sally's arm, nudging her awake.

'Look at the swing,' he said to her. 'What do you see?'

Sally opened her eyes and lifted her sunglasses to look into the tree's shadow better. She shook her head. 'All I see is Sophie.'

'You don't see another girl with her?'

'No, I don't.' She called to Sophie. 'Sophie! Sophie! Come here, please.'

Sophie got off the swing and made her way towards the pair of them. Ben continued to look at the swing. The other girl had disappeared.

'Who were you talking to, Sophie?'

'Nobody,' she said, swinging from side to side and looking a little coy.

Sally smiled and turned to Ben. 'See. No one.'

'Who's your friend, Sophie?'

Sophie seemed slightly reluctant to reply, still swinging from side to side.

'It's okay. You can tell us, pumpkin,' Sally said, not expecting anything further but humouring Ben.

'She told me not to say anything,' Sophie confided.

Sally sat up. That was not the expected response.

'What did she tell you to say?' Ben said.

'That she lives here as well.'

'Have you seen her before?'

Sophie nodded. 'We play together in the bedroom sometimes.'

'And how long has this been going on?' Sally said, a little harder than necessary.

Sophie shrugged. 'Long time.'

'What's her name, Sophie, because I've also seen her.'

'Mattie,' Sophie said.

'Okay, off you go and play, then.'

Sophie skipped off down the garden to the old oak again.

'Now, do you believe me?' Ben said when Sophie was out of earshot.

'She's just a young girl making up stories about an invisible friend.'

Ben stood, lowering his voice.

'Fuck's sake, Sally. You've never believed, even when you've seen it with your own eyes, and you don't believe your daughter.'

'No, I don't. It's your overactive imagination.' Sally rolled off the sunbed she'd been lying on and stormed into the house.

Dark clouds had formed over the Strait of Dover, and thunder rumbled in the distance.

Sally entered the kitchen and filled a glass with ice water from the fridge. She heard a noise behind her and turned to see that Ben had followed her into the house.

'I'm sorry, Ben. I can't believe all this mumbo-jumbo.'

'Open your mind, Sally. There is more to life than this mortal existence.'

'So you say.'

'Yes, I say.'

The rain came.

And more rain came. For three weeks, work on Cloverleaf House's new conservatory stalled. When it eventually dried up, Ben was sitting in his office when he got a call from the foreman of the workers on site. He said, 'You need to come and see what we've found here.'

Ben, wondering whether they'd found another unexploded World War Two bomb, went downstairs and to the side of the house.

'What's up, then?' he asked the foreman, who indicated for him to follow. He then pointed to the corner of the area they were digging out for the footings. In the corner was a small skull.

Weeks after the child's skull was found, the detective inspector in charge visited Ben and Sally. It was time they had some news. Ben had been fretting over the lack of information coming from the police. They'd kept away from the goings-on by the forensic people at the side of the house. The only thing they knew for sure was that not only were the remains of a child found, but also those of an adult male. Ben had his suspicions but kept them to himself.

After settling in the kitchen with coffee and biscuits, Ben said, 'What's the news then, Inspector?'

The DI took a sip from his mug. 'I can tell you we have done all we can at the site, so our forensic teams will pack up and move off-site today.'

'Does that mean we can carry on with our conservatory?' Sally asked.

The DI nodded and took another sip from his mug.

'What can you tell us about the remains?' Ben asked.

'Well, they have been there since the wartime bombing. There is fire damage on both sets of remains, and they've been carbon-dated to the 1940s. We also know that the damage to the remains is consistent with crush injuries, with no suspicious indicators of foul play.'

'Do you believe them to be the occupants of the house during the time?' Sally said.

'I do, yes.'

'Our research suggested that two of the four who perished in the fire were never found.'

'Then I think you may have answered the only remaining question. Who were they?' The DI continued. 'Our enquiries show that the male remains are one Frederick Winters, and the child would be Alice Martinique.'

'She was the twelve-year-old?' Ben asked.

'Correct.'

'What happened to the other little girl ... Mattie?' Sally asked.

'I did some old-fashioned legwork,' the DI said. 'And I had a look at some local records. Mattie, or Matilda Martinique, is buried in the local churchyard. I went there, and there's a headstone for her. Her parents are also in the church.'

'So, can we have the remains, Inspector?'

'To put them to rest with the sister and parents? I don't see why not.'

'What about Fred Winters?' Ben asked. 'I couldn't find much about him in the archive.'

'There is a story to him, from what I've discovered,' the DI said.

'Do you normally go to all this bother, Inspector?' Sally said.

'No, but I have an interest in local history.'

'Fred,' prompted Ben.

'Ah ... Fred was a bit of a local hero, it seems. Served in the Kent Light Infantry during World War One, and got himself a Distinguished Service Cross. Got gassed. Demobbed met his future wife, Molly—'

'They were married?' interrupted Ben.

The DI nodded.

'We didn't know that,' Ben said.

'There was some connection between the Martiniques, taken into their employ as a temporary gesture but stayed.

'Where's his wife?'

'In the same churchyard.'

Ben and Sally nodded in satisfaction. 'Then we can put them all to rest together.'

'That sounds like a plan to me,' the DI said. 'I'll make the arrangements and be in touch.'

Ben saw the DI out.

BY NOW, Sally was heavily pregnant with number three. She had taken early maternity leave from work, so she was at home alone while Ben went to work, taking the children to school as he did so.

She was sitting in the lounge, listening to some soothing music, when suddenly the door to the room crashed open.

There was the thunder of feet running around the room and children laughing. The room went quiet. Then the door banged shut. This was not the first time this had happened since she'd been alone in the house. She'd not said anything to Ben about it. She knew who it was. She knew who they were and felt that these spooky goings-on would end after they had laid the remains to rest.

Today, though, things were different. It wasn't just the laughing and playing children that she could cope with; other things that had happened over the last few days began to worry her. Her things would go missing, not because she had forgotten where they were.

The entire atmosphere in the house had changed to something more sinister.

ALSO BY STEPHEN COLLIER

ABOUT THE AUTHOR

Stephen Collier is a retired police officer and business owner. He is a crime fiction author and an independent publisher. He has published three crime fiction books and a book written by his late aunt, Ruth Martin.

Stephen lives in Northamptonshire, UK, with his partner Sarah. He can be reached for talks and seminars at: -

www.stephencollier.com/contact